The Affairs of Sherlock Holmes

By

Sax Rohmer

Volume I

• • •

Edited by

Alan Lance Andersen

First edition published in 2016

Paperback ISBN 978-1-78705-000-6
ePub ISBN 978-1-78705-001-3
PDF ISBN 978-1-78705-002-0

Published in the UK by MX Publishing
335 Princess Park Manor, Royal Drive,
London, N11 3GX
www.mxpublishing.co.uk

Cover compiled by Brian Belanger

INTRODUCTION

Sax Rohmer, the pen name of Arthur Sarsfield Ward, is best known today for his blood-and-thunder mysteries involving the insidious Chinese mastermind — Fu Manchu. These stories, first published in magazines, were subsequently made into movies, radio dramas, theatre dramas, television shows, and published books.

Less known (but perhaps better written) were Rohmer's stories of Bazarada — who was based on Rohmer's friend Harry Houdini, as evidenced by this quotation from *The Jade Serpent:* "Locks meant less than nothing to Bazarada; no prison bars could cage him. Men of first-class intelligence credited him with occult powers. And those who were present when, handcuffed and leg-ironed in a sealed wine cask, he was lowered into the Rhine at Duesseldorf, will remember the moment when he swam to the surface. My own seal, amongst others, was intact on the cask when we hauled it up. Inside, we found the manacles and leg-irons ..."

And then there were Rohmer's tales of Chinatown from 1916. These were set in the London Limehouse district near the Thames docks, as opposed to the better-known San Francisco Chinatown or the ones in New York City, Los Angeles, Vancouver, Chicago, Toronto, Boston, Philadelphia, Detroit, and Montreal; as well as international Chinatowns in Manila, Nagasaki, and elsewhere. Unlike San Francisco's Chinatown, London's is NOT a tourist destination. In Rohmer's day, it was an unwholesome slum with a warren of dark narrow streets and shadowy alleyways, derelict warehouses, dangerous taverns, and opium dens. Limehouse before the first World War housed an Asian community, largely criminal, which lived by foreign laws more ancient than the laws of England.

It was an area in which Rohmer loved to go "slumming" — and he made lifelong friends of many of the Chinese who lived there. It was on a dark and foggy night in Limehouse, in an alley off a dingy street near the canal, that Sax Rohmer had a *very brief glimpse* of the Chinese crime lord that ruled London's Chinatown in 1911, and it nearly scared him to death. He said the man was the living embodiment of Satan. It was this "King of Chinatown," master of gambling houses, cocaine, and opium who served as Rohmer's model for the character Fu Manchu.

In the late 1800s and early 1900s, at the peak of Sherlock Holmes' popularity, a number of writers wrote their own mystery stories that were in many ways similar to Holmes. Many of Sax Rohmer's little-known stories read, but for the names and places, almost exactly like Arthur Conan Doyle's original Sherlock Holmes stories — in fact, much of the language is more like the original Holmes canon than most stories written by modern authors. Rohmer was also a much better writer than many of the other "Rivals of Sherlock Holmes" authors.

The editor of this volume has carefully edited some of Rohmer's best Chinatown tales into Sherlock Holmes pastiches.

PREFACE

Rivals of Conan Doyle:

Inherent Problems for Modern Authors Writing Sherlock Holmes Pastiches

By Alan Lance Andersen

Modern authors from John Dickson Carr to Nicholas Meyer have attempted to recapture the mood of gaslit London and the mystique of Sir Arthur Conan Doyle's adventures of Sherlock Holmes by writing "new" Holmes novels and short stories. Such authors usually seize upon certain elements of the Holmes canon — the tobacco in the slipper, the violin, the use of cocaine — to lend an air of verisimilitude to their "Victorian" stories. Yet these attempts invariably fail to capture the original flavor of the Conan Doyle tales.

On the other hand, Conan Doyle's contemporaries — such mystery authors as Robert Eustace, L.T. Meade, Clifford Halifax, Richard Harding Davis, and Sax Rohmer (whose stories are featured in this volume) — were writing about characters of their own invention; nevertheless they sound more like Conan Doyle than do any of his modern deliberate imitators. It is my belief that this results from the Victorians sharing a common linguistic and rhetorical background, world view, and social mind-set which later writers can never fully understand. Writers of "new" Victorian mysteries would do well to focus on the language and societal culture of the period rather than on furniture and dress; and they should avoid having characters behave in ways which, clever though they may be in terms of plot, are nevertheless out-of-character for a 19th Century writer to include in a story.

• • •

Most mystery writers acknowledge Edgar Allan Poe and Sir Arthur Conan Doyle for their roles in the development of the mystery story as we know it today. Throughout the history of detective literature, there have been outstanding writers whose works have helped to shape the mystery genre. Beginning in 1891, the *Strand Magazine* began featuring a Sherlock Holmes short story in each issue, which assured instant success for the new publication. Prior to that time, there had been only two Holmes tales, both novels. The first, *A Study in Scarlet*, was published in *Beeton's Christmas Annual* in 1887 and the second, *The Sign of the Four*, was published in *Lippincott's Magazine* in 1890.

It was with the publication of "A Scandal in Bohemia" in *The Strand Magazine* in July 1991 that stories really caught on. They made Conan Doyle's career and catapulted *The Strand Magazine* to the position of premier periodical of its day. It was not long before other writers of short mystery fiction began to appear in *Pearson's Magazine, Cassell's Magazine, The Harmsworth Magazine, The Royal Magazine, The Windsor Magazine, The Ludgate Monthly,* and *The London Magazine* — as well as in *The Strand Magazine*. Such authors included L. T. Meade, Robert Eustace, Clifford Halifax, Jacques Futrelle, Baroness Orczy, Brett Harte, Jack London, Guy Boothby, Arthur Morrison, E. W. Hornung, William McHarg, Edwin Balmer, Samuel Hopkins Adams, Francis Lynde, Catherine Louisa Pirkis, William Hope Hodgson, Ernest Bramah, Richard Harding Davis, Robert Barr, Cutcliffe Hyne, Grant Allen, and Sarsfield Ward (before *and* after he took the pen name of Sax Rohmer). These authors created their own characters — detectives and master criminals — and the first golden age of mystery writing began.

A number of modern writers have undertaken to write their own Sherlock Holmes mysteries, yet none of these recent stories has ever fully captured the quality and flavor of the original. Eric Zorn writes in the Chicago *Tribune*, "One can scarcely turn around in a bookstore without seeing (Holmes) rocketing into space, solving President Kennedy's assassination, or consorting with clones and vampires ... Modern writers, using all the gimmicks at their disposal, seem determined to cash in on the late Arthur Conan Doyle's work."

Even if we discount the science fiction and fantasy writers of Sherlock Holmes stories and focus on those honestly trying to recreate the style and tone of the original canon, we find that modern authors invariably fail to capture the flavor of the Conan Doyle stories. They use the "trappings" of Sherlock Holmes — the tobacco in the slipper, the violin, the use of cocaine — to lend an air of verisimilitude to their "Victorian" stories. But these imitators often attempt to introduce ideas of their own which are not consistent with late Victorian times, language, or literary conventions.

Other modern writers have written period mysteries set in 19th Century England using their own characters or fictionalized versions of historical figures. Some of these stories are quite successful in recreating Victorian-seeming prose, while others fall into the same traps as the Conan Doyle imitators.

5

Among the better known of the latter-day Sherlock Holmes novels are Nicholas Meyer's *The Seven-Per-Cent Solution* and *The West End Horror*. Meyer's stories are intriguing, his knowledge of Holmes is thorough, and his attention to detail is excellent. The main problem with these stories is that Meyer is an inveterate name-dropper. He insists on peopling his stories with such famous figures as Sigmund Freud, Oscar Wilde, and George Bernard Shaw.

While Holmes would certainly have had dealings with celebrities like Wilde and Shaw, Conan Doyle would never have actually named them in a story; he would have used euphemisms like "a notorious poet" or "a celebrated playwright." In *The West End Horror*, Holmes is called in to help capture Jack the Ripper. Perhaps the worst example of this is a scene in *The Seven-Per-Cent Solution* with a cameo appearance by a character from Anthony Hope's *The Prisoner of Zenda*. This plays no part whatsoever in the story; it simply gives Meyer the opportunity to footnote, "Here is one of the great accidental meetings in recent English history, pregnant with all sorts of irony."

The fact is that Conan Doyle never mentions real people by name in his stories. It was a matter of Victorian reserve to be subtle about such things. Conan Doyle features the King of Bohemia in one of his tales, at about the same time that Robert Louis Stevenson was writing stories in the *New Arabian Nights* about Prince Florizel of Bohemia — who in turn was helped in solving a mystery by "a celebrated London detective." Conan Doyle and Stevenson were correspondents at this time, and "borrowed" each others characters. But it would have been in poor taste to name them. Good taste was everything to a Victorian gentleman.

Conan Doyle might have had Dr. Watson come home to find Holmes taking cocaine, but he would never have been so indiscreet as to *quote* Holmes' unfortunate language while under the influence. But in Michael Hardwick's *Revenge of the Hound,* an entire chapter is devoted to describing Holmes' aberrant behavior and his berating of Watson during a cocaine session. This so shatters the familiar image of Holmes' and Watson's domestic scene that it ruins the rest of the book. One of the things that makes the Sherlock Holmes stories so endearing to readers are the glimpses of domestic life at 221B Baker Street, and Hardwick totally failed to capture that mood.

The biggest problem with many modern Sherlock Holmes stories is that the author comes up with his own pet notions about Holmes and tries to be cute in his portrayal. For example, in *The Private Life of Sherlock Holmes,* Holmes asserts that he and Watson were homosexual lovers. Even if that were true — which it is NOT — Holmes would never say anything about it. If one is going to write stories using someone else's characters, the least one can do is be faithful to the original.

Another problem for the modern writer is that the English language has changed considerably since Victorian times. While we can read and easily understand Victorian prose, we tend not to *think* in that style, which makes writing it difficult. Furthermore, phrases that sound perfectly normal to us may not have even been used back then. In the recent television production of *Jack the Ripper,* which is set in 1888, Michael Caine starring as Detective Inspector Frederick Abberline says to another character, "Shut your face." According to Wenworth and Flexner's *Dictionary of American Slang*, this figure of speech was not used until after 1915, and it is an American expression — not British.

Such anachronisms, while subtle, can create an overall effect in which the story simply does not "ring true."

Zorn writes, "Revival pastiches typically have been greeted with hoots of derision from true Sherlockians, a righteous bunch who do not suffer gladly transgressions upon the sacred memory of Holmes and Dr. Watson."

A good way to get a feel for authentic Victorian language is to read Castle Books' *Rivals of Sherlock Holmes*, a two-volume facsimile edition of original mystery stories from *Strand Magazine, Windsor Magazine, The Royal Magazine,* and other publications from the era of gaslight and hansom cabs. These stories, written by the 19th century writers listed above, read very much like those of Sir Arthur Conan Doyle. One sees numerous similarities in style — and these are the hallmarks of late Victorian prose. One will also be able to pick out the elements of Conan Doyle's personal writing style, for they stand out distinctly once one is steeped in the language of the period. The original illustrations reproduced in these facsimile editions also help create a feeling for the Victorian era.

One of the best of the "rivals" is Richard Harding Davis' "In the Fog," a trilogy of short stories originally published in *The Windsor Magazine.* A group of gentlemen at a private London club regale each other with tales of a convoluted mystery that so engages the interest of Sir Andrew, an elderly gentleman and devoted Sherlock Holmes fan, that he fails to depart for the House of Lords to make a speech on the Navy Increase Bill. The surprise ending of this story is a true Victorian masterpiece.

The prolific L.T. Meade, one of the foremost women mystery writers of the time, collaborated with Dr. Edgar

Beaumont to write a series of stories in which Dr. Clifford Hallifax (Beaumont's pseudonym) solves a number of insidious crimes. With Robert Eustace, she penned a trilogy of stories about Madame Sarah, "The Sorceress of the Strand" — a villainess to rival Conan Doyle's Professor Moriarty.

Some late Victorian mysteries featured the villain as a protagonist who habitually outwitted the police. E. W. Hornung's cricketer and notorious master thief A. J. Raffles was so popular that the series was continued by other writers after Hornung's death.

Baroness Orczy — better known, perhaps, for her tales of the adventurous and heroic Scarlet Pimpernel — penned a series of stories about Patrick "Skin O' My Tooth" Mulligan, a lawyer with a reputation for winning particularly close criminal court cases.

All of these mystery stories — and those found in other anthologies — illustrate the style of writing, the social attitudes, and the literary conventions of the late Victorian and Edwardian period. There is a naive freshness to these stories and a mystique not easily captured by modern writers.

The most "successful" of Conan Doyle's plagiarists was a contemporary unemployed architect by the name of Arthur Whitaker, whose story, *The Man Who Was Wanted,* was subsequently believed by Adrian and Denis Conan Doyle to have been written by their father. The story of literary feuding and fiascoes that surrounded the publication of Arthur Whitaker's story is presented in its entirety in Jon L. Lellenberg's *Nova 57 Minor.*

Unlike Sir Arthur's modern imitators, Whitaker wrote his Holmes story at the same time that Conan Doyle was at the peak of his popularity; and there is a ring of authenticity in the narrative that modern imitators are lacking. Still, Whitaker's story might never have seen the light of day were it not for a series of misadventures which led to his manuscript being discovered among Sir Arthur's papers after his death — *with no mention of the typescript's origin!*

Although Whitaker's attempt to imitate Conan Doyle's literary style was more successful than those of modern imitators, it did not feel quite right to Holmes aficionados. Whitaker wrote the story in the *style of the period* and included *all the traditional trappings* of a Sherlock Holmes story, but his *personal writing style* differed from Sir Arthur's! This was lost on sons Adrian Conan Doyle and Denis Conan Doyle (who not only deified their father's memory but who had also reportedly been paid $15,000 for the story) — but it was not lost on daughter Jean Conan Doyle. Lellenberg says Jean was certain *The Man Who Was Wanted* was not written by her father when she first read the story in the *Sunday Dispatch*, and that she was put out with her brother Adrian for not telling her of it's impending publication.

Lellenberg writes "Adrian lacked the special knowledge, or insight, or prescience (or whatever it is) of the dyed-in-the-wool enthusiast ... for whom the story did not 'ring true.' Some have that sensitivity, while others do not. Only one of Conan Doyle's children had it, and she had not been consulted."

Adrian Conan Doyle was adamant in his denunciation of writers who "plagiarized" his father's characters. Lellenberg describes Adrian preventing Ellery Queen from publishing an anthology of Sherlockian parodies and pastiches. A promising series of Holmes pastiches by mystery writer Stuart Palmer was "nipped in the bud" when "the legal heirs of the late Sir Arthur Conan Doyle set up shrill wails of agony at the very idea of the continuance of the series."

Adrian described his views on plagiarism and the Whitaker story in a letter to Vincent Starrett:

"Is it not infuriating that one can be put to so much trouble and inconvenience, after 40 years, thanks directly to the abominable habit of a would-be writer in making use of characters invented by an established Author."

Considering his attitude, it is amusing to note that Adrian Conan Doyle himself subsequently wrote a series of Sherlock Holmes stories in collaboration with John Dickson Carr in the 1940s. These stories have interesting mystery plots and are fairly constrained in their adherence to the original format, yet they are flawed. John Dickson Carr's writing style is so forceful that his personality comes through in spite of his efforts to imitate Sir Arthur.

In a review of Edward B. Hanna's *The Whitechapel Horrors,* another book in which Holmes is called in to help capture Jack the Ripper, Bruce Southworth points out that book's shortcomings (*Once Upon a Crime,* Vol. 1, No. 4). At one point early in *The Whitechapel Horrors,* Watson espouses the out-of-character sentiment that "the poor are poor because they're deserving of nothing better. They could rise above their station if they wished ... Those who choose to live like animals do so because they are animals." Southworth point out that this quote colors the rest of the book.

In another passage, Holmes mutters a celebrated modern obscenity. According to Southworth, this is "Not an uncommon word nowadays, but (one) which, in my almost 25 years of involvement with the adventures of Holmes, and the 'writings about the writings,' is a first."

It is very doubtful whether the word in question was used in that fashion in Victorian England. It was never used in print when I was a boy; Watson would certainly never have quoted Holmes — even if he *had* said it.

Southworth writes, "It is an extensively researched and well-written Ripper novel. As for Hanna's efforts to write a Holmes novel, this must be judged a failure. If you ... pretend that the characters of Holmes, Watson, Mycroft, *et al.* are other than those created by Doyle, you will enjoy *The Whitechapel Horrors.* If you are a Holmesian purist, this is not the book for you." By this standard, *The Man Who Was Wanted* is a success, for the characters are very true to the canon. Southworth further points out, "Sir Arthur Conan Doyle advised would-be pastiche writers to invent their own characters rather than use his. Hanna should have heeded the sage advice from the man who knew Holmes best, his creator."

This final statement refers to Conan Doyle's letter to Whitaker (reproduced in *Nova 57 Minor),* wherein Sir Arthur writes of *The Man Who Was Wanted,* "You should ... change the names and try to get published yourself. Of course you could not use the names of my characters."

It is the modern authors who take Sir Arthur's advice that are most successful. Victorian mystery stories were very much formula writing, and were sometimes rather stuffy and naive. By combining the Victorian style with modern plot and characterization, it is possible to come up with stories that are even better than some of the originals.

A particularly successful period novel is Peter Lovesey's *Bertie and the Tinman*, which actually reads as though it were written by a gentleman of the 1880s, but which has more excitement and humor than is usually found in the writing of that period. In this case, the detective is Albert Edward, the Prince of Wales and future King of England. Since Lovesey is not attempting to imitate another writer's style of writing, the use of a historical figure as the hero is appropriate.

Another noteworthy period novel is *The Detective and Mr. Dickens*, by modern author W. J. Palmer, in which Charles Dickens and Wilkie Collins are enlisted to help Inspector Field — a Bow Street policeman found in Dickens' sketches in *Household Words* — to solve a murder committed by a group of "gentlemen." Dickens and Collins are able to enter London's private clubs to gather information where Inspector Field would never be accepted. The tale is presented as "a secret journal" supposedly penned by Wilkie Collins after Dickens' death.

While quite successful at recreating the world of gaslit London, both *Bertie and the Tinman* and *The Detective and Mr. Dickens* suffer from a problem common to many modern writers of Victorian and Edwardian novels. They are much more explicit in describing sexual details than any 19th Century writer would have been. This is a matter of propriety. We know that there were rakes and libertines in the 19th Century, but writers of that period would have used euphemisms, vagueness, or pretended innocence rather than offend public sensibilities. This matter of propriety and taste were so codified in Victorian times that the euphemisms and phraseology actually became part of the literary style.

Historical novels with flaws in fact or style are painful to the knowledgeable reader, but well-crafted period mysteries that pay attention to style and detail are often among the very best writing in the mystery genre.

A very young A. Sarsfield Ward wrote the science fiction murder mystery "The Green Spider" in 1904, years before creating the most infamous villain of mystery fiction, Fu Manchu, under the pen name of Sax Rohmer. He was also the creator of Bazarada — a mystery solving magician based on Harry Houdini. Many of his later detective mysteries were so like Sherlock Holmes that — with the names and locations changed — they read more like late Victorian Holmes pastiches than those penned by modern writers who try so hard to write like Conan Doyle.

The stories in this book are mystery tales by Sax Rohmer carefully edited to turn them into Sherlock Holmes pastiches.

CONTENTS

The Affair of the White Silk Hat

The Affair of the Barber Atrocity

The Affair of the Chinaman's Pigtail

The Affair of the Golden Idol

NOTICE

This Book is Prepared Entirely from Public Domain sources.
No Copyrighted Materials were used in this Project.

The Affair of the White Silk Hat

I.

MAJOR JACK RAGSTAFF

"Hallo! Mrs. Hudson," said Sherlock Holmes as our landlady at 221B Baker Street knocked at the door. "Someone is making a devil of a row downstairs."

"This is the offender, Mr. Holmes," said Mrs. Hudson, and handed my friend a visiting card.

Glancing at the card, Holmes read aloud:

"Major J. E. P. Ragstaff, Cavalry Club."

Meanwhile a loud harsh voice, which would have been audible in a full gale, was roaring in the lobby.

"Nonsense!" I could hear the Major shouting. "Balderdash! There's more fuss than if I had asked for an interview with the Prime Minister. Piffle! Balderdash!"

Mrs. Hudson's smile developed into a laugh, in which Holmes joined, then:

"Admit the Major," he said.

Into the study where Holmes and I had been seated quietly smoking, there presently strode a very choleric Anglo-Indian. He wore a horsy check suit and white spats, and his tie closely resembled a stock. In his hand he carried a heavy malacca cane, gloves, and one of those tall, light-gray hats commonly termed white. He was below medium height, slim and wiry; his gait and the shape of his legs, his build, all proclaimed the dragoon. His complexion was purple, and the large white teeth visible beneath a bristling gray moustache added to the natural ferocity of his appearance. Standing just within the doorway:

"Mr. Sherlock Holmes?" he shouted.

It was apparently an inquiry, but it sounded like a reprimand.

My friend, standing before the fireplace, his hands in his pockets and his pipe in his mouth, nodded brusquely.

"I am Sherlock Holmes," he said. "Won't you sit down?"

Major Ragstaff, glancing angrily at Mrs. Hudson as the latter left the study, tossed his stick and gloves on to a settee, and drawing up a chair seated himself stiffly upon it as though he were in a saddle. He stared straight at Holmes.

"You are not the sort of person I expected, sir," he declared. "May I ask if it is your custom to keep clients dancin' on the mat and all that — on the blasted mat, sir?"

Holmes suppressed a smile, and I hastily reached for my cigarette-case which I had placed upon the mantel-shelf.

"I am always naturally pleased to see clients, Major Ragstaff," said Holmes, "but a certain amount of routine is necessary even in civilian life. You had not advised me of your visit, and it is contrary to my custom to discuss business after five o'clock."

As Holmes spoke, the Major glared at him continuously, and then:

"I've seen you before!" he roared; "bless me! I've seen you before! — yes! in Switzerland! Ha! I've got you now sir!" He sprang to his feet. "You're the Sherlock Holmes who fell off Reichenback Falls back in 18__ "

"Quite true."

"I thought you were dead."

"That remains to be seen, Major."

"But I am told you are now a consulting detective, and all that."

"So I am," said Holmes quietly. "I am now at the service of anyone who cares to employ me."

"Thunderation!" said the Major.

He seemed to be temporarily stricken speechless. Staring all about the room with a sort of naive wonderment, he drew out a big silk handkerchief and loudly blew his nose, all the time eyeing Holmes questioningly. Replacing his handkerchief he directed his regard upon me.

"This is my friend, Dr. Watson," said Sherlock Holmes; "you may state your case before him without hesitation, unless — "

I rose to depart, but:

"Sit down, Dr. Watson! Sit down, sir!" shouted the Major. "I have no dirty linen to wash, no skeletons in the cupboard or piffle of that kind. I simply want something explained which I am too thick-headed — too demmed thick-headed, sir — to explain myself."

He resumed his seat, and taking out his wallet extracted from it a small newspaper cutting which he offered to Holmes.

"Read that, Mr. Holmes," he directed. "Read it aloud."

Holmes read as follows:

> "Before Mr. Smith, at Marlborough Street Police Court, John Edward Bampton was charged with assaulting a well-known clubman in Bond Street on Wednesday evening. It was proved by the constable who made the arrest that robbery had not been the motive of the assault, and Bampton confessed that he bore no grudge against the assailed man, indeed, that he had never seen him before. He pleaded intoxication, and the police surgeon testified that although not actually intoxicated, his breath had smelled strongly of liquor at the time of his arrest. Bampton's employers testified to a hitherto blameless character, and as the charge was not pressed the man was dismissed with a caution."

Having read the paragraph, Holmes glanced at the Major with a puzzled expression.

"The point of this quite escapes me," he confessed.

"Is that so?" said Major Ragstaff. "Is that so, sir? Perhaps you will be good enough to read this."

From his wallet he took a second newspaper cutting, smaller than the first, and gummed to a sheet of club notepaper. Holmes took it and read as follows:

> "Mr. De Lana, a well-known member of the Stock Exchange, who met with a serious accident recently, is still in a precarious condition."

The puzzled look on Holmes's face grew more acute, and the Major watched him with an expression which I can only describe as one of fierce enjoyment.

"You're thinkin' I'm a demmed old fool, ain't you?" he shouted suddenly.

"Scarcely that," said Holmes, smiling slightly, "but the significance of these paragraphs is not apparent, I must confess. The man Bampton would not appear to be an interesting character, and since no great damage has been done, his drunken frolic hardly comes within my sphere. Of Mr. De Lana, of the Stock Exchange, I never heard, unless he happens to be a member of the firm of De Lana and Day?"

"He's *not* a member of that firm, sir," shouted the Major. "He *was* ... up to six o'clock this evenin'."

"What do you mean exactly?" inquired Holmes, and the tone of his voice suggested that he was beginning to entertain doubts of the Major's sanity or sobriety; then:

"He's dead!" declared the latter. "Dead as the Begum of Bangalore! He died at six o'clock. I've just had a telegram from his widow."

I suppose I must have been staring very hard at the speaker, and certainly Holmes was doing so, for suddenly directing his fierce gaze toward me:

"You're completely treed, sir, and so's your friend!" shouted Major Ragstaff.

"I confess it," replied Holmes quietly; "and since my time is of some little value I would suggest, without disrespect, that you explain the connection, if any, between yourself, the drunken Bampton, and Mr. De Lana, of the Stock Exchange, who died, you inform us, at six o'clock this evening as the result, presumably, of injuries received in an accident."

"That's what I'm here for!" cried Major Ragstaff. "In the first place, then, I am the party, although I saw to it that my name was kept out of print, whom the drunken lunatic assaulted."

Holmes, pipe in hand, stared at the speaker perplexedly.

"Understand me," continued the Major, "I am the person — I, Jack Ragstaff — he assaulted. I was walkin' down from my quarters in Maddox Street on my way to dine at the club, same as I do every night o' my life, when this flamin' idiot sprang upon me, grabbed my hat" — he took up his white silk hat to illustrate what had occurred — "not this one, but one like it — pitched it on the ground and jumped on it!"

Holmes was quite unable to conceal his smiles as the excited old soldier dropped his conspicuous head-gear on the floor

24

and indulged in a vigorous pantomime designed to illustrate his statement.

"Most extraordinary," said Holmes. "What did you do?"

"What did I do?" roared the Major. "I gave him a crack on the head with my cane, and I said things to him which couldn't be repeated in court. I punched him, and likewise hoofed him, but the hat was completely done in. Blasted crowd collected, hearin' me swearin' and bellowin'. Police and all that; names an' addresses and all that balderdash. Man lugged away to guard-room and me turnin' up at the club with no hat. Dashed ridiculous spectacle at my time of life."

"Quite so," said Holmes soothingly; "I appreciate your annoyance, but I am utterly at a loss to understand why you have come here, and what all this has to do with Mr. De Lana, of the Stock Exchange."

"He fell out of the window!" shouted the Major.

"Fell out of a window?"

"Out of a window, sir, a second floor window ten yards up a side street! Pitched on his skull — marvel he wasn't killed outright!"

A faint expression of interest began to creep into Holmes's glance.

"I understand you to mean, Major Ragstaff," he said deliberately, "that while your struggle with the drunken man was in progress, Mr. De Lana fell out of a neighbouring window into the street?"

"Right!" shouted the Major. "Right, sir!"

"Do you know this Mr. De Lana?"

"Never heard of him in my life until the accident occurred. Seems to me the poor devil leaned out to see the fun and overbalanced. Felt responsible, only natural, and made inquiries. He died at six o'clock this evenin', sir."

"H'm," said Holmes reflectively. "I still fail to see where I come in. From what window did he fall?"

"Window above a sort of teashop, called Café Dame — dashed silly name. Place on a corner. Don't know name of side street."

"Hmm. You don't think he was pushed out, for instance?"

"Certainly not!" shouted the Major. "He just fell out, but the point is, he's dead!"

"My dear sir," said Holmes patiently, "I don't dispute that point; but what on earth do you want of me?"

"I don't know what I want!" roared the Major, beginning to walk up and down the room, "but I know I ain't satisfied, not easy in my mind, sir. I wake up of a night hearin' the poor devil's yell as he crashed on the pavement. That's all wrong. I've heard hundreds of death-yells, but" — he took up his malacca cane and beat it loudly on the table — "I haven't woke up of a night dreamin' I heard 'em again."

"In a word, you suspect foul play?"

"I don't suspect anything!" cried the other excitedly, "but someone mentioned your name to me at the club — said you could see through concrete, and all that — and here I am. There's something wrong, radically wrong. Find out what it is and send the bill to me. Then perhaps I'll be able to sleep in peace."

He paused, and again taking out the large silk handkerchief blew his nose loudly. Holmes glanced at me in rather an odd way, and then:

"There will be no bill, Major Ragstaff," he said; "but if I can see any possible line of inquiry I will pursue it and report the result to you."

II.

A CURIOUS OUTRAGE

"What do you make of it, Holmes?" I asked. Sherlock Holmes returned a work of reference to its shelf and stood staring absently across the study.

"Our late visitor's history does not help us much," he replied. "A somewhat distinguished army career, and so forth, and his only daughter, Sybil Margaret, married the fifth Marquis of Ireton. She is, therefore, the noted society beauty, the Marchioness of Ireton. Does this suggest anything to your mind?"

"Nothing whatever," I said blankly.

"Nor to mine," murmured Holmes.

The doorbell rang.

"Hallo!" called Holmes and the door opened. It was a young street urchin employed by Holmes to run errands. The youth was holding a cable. "Yes, thank you, Billy. From Lestrade? Let's see. Splendid. Here's sixpence, Billy. Many thanks."

Holmes turned to me.

"I suggest, Watson," he said, "that we make our call and then proceed to dinner as arranged."

Since I was always glad of an opportunity of studying my friend's methods, I immediately agreed; and ere long, leaving the lights of the two big hotels behind, our hansom was gliding down the long slope which leads to Waterloo Station. Thence through crowded, slummish high-roads we made our way *via* Lambeth to that dismal thoroughfare, Westminster Bridge Road, with its forbidding, often windowless, houses, and its peculiar air of desolation.

The house for which we were bound was situated at no great distance from Kensington Park, and telling the hansom driver to wait, Holmes and I walked up a narrow, paved path, mounted a flight of steps, and rang the bell beside a somewhat time-worn door, above which was an old-fashioned fanlight dimly illuminated from within.

A considerable interval elapsed before the door was opened by a marvellously untidy servant girl who had apparently been interrupted in the act of black-leading her face. Partly opening the door, she stared at us agape, pushing back wisps of hair from her eyes and with every movement daubing more of some mysterious black substance upon her countenance.

"Is Mr. Bampton in?" asked Holmes.

"Yus, just come in. I'm cookin' his supper."

"Tell him that two friends of his have called on rather important business."

"All right," said the black-faced one. "What name is it?"

"No name. Just say two friends of his."

Treating us to a long, vacant stare and leaving us standing on the step, the maid (in whose hand I perceived a greasy fork) shuffled along the passage and began to mount the stairs. An unmistakable odour of frying sausages now reached my nostrils. Holmes glanced at me quizzically, but said nothing until the Cinderella came stumbling downstairs again, without returning to where we stood.

"Go on up," she directed. "Second floor, front. Shut the door, one of yer."

She disappeared into gloomy depths below as Holmes and I, closing the door behind us, proceeded to avail ourselves of the invitation. There was very little light on the staircase, but we managed to find our way to a poorly furnished bed-sitting room where a small table was spread for a meal. Beside the table, in a chintz-covered armchair, a thick-set young man was seated smoking a cigarette and having a copy of the *Daily Telegraph* upon his knees.

He was a very typical lower middle-class, nothing-in-particular young man, but there was a certain truculence indicated by his square jaw, and that sort of self-possession which sometimes accompanies physical strength was evidenced in his manner as, tossing the paper aside, he stood up.

"Good evening, Mr. Bampton," said Holmes genially. "I take it" — pointing to the newspaper — "that you are looking for a new job?"

Bampton stared, a suspicion of anger in his eyes, then, meeting the amused glance of my friend, he broke into a smile very pleasing and humorous. He was a fresh-coloured young fellow with hair inclined to redness, and smiling he looked very boyish indeed.

"I have no idea who you are," he said, speaking with a faint north-country accent, "but you evidently know who I am and what has happened to me."

"Got the boot?" asked Holmes confidentially.

Bampton, tossing the end of his cigarette into the grate, nodded grimly.

"You haven't told me your name," he said, "but I think I can tell you your business." He ceased smiling. "Now look here, I don't want any more publicity. If you think you are going to make a funny newspaper story out of me, you can change your mind as quick as you like. I'll never get another job in London as it is. If you drag me any further into the limelight, I'll never get another job in England."

"My dear fellow," replied Holmes soothingly, at the same time extending his cigarette-case, "you misapprehend the object of my call. I am not a reporter."

"What!" said Bampton, pausing in the act of taking a cigarette, "then what the devil are you?"

"My name is Sherlock Holmes, and I am a criminal investigator."

He spoke the words deliberately, having his eyes fixed upon the other's face; but although Bampton was palpably startled there was no trace of fear in his straightforward glance. He took a cigarette from the case.

"Thanks, Mr. Holmes," he said. "I cannot imagine what business has brought you here."

"I have come to ask you two questions," was the reply. "Number one: Who paid you to smash Major Ragstaff's white hat? Number two: How much did he pay you?"

To these questions I listened in amazement, and my amazement was evidently shared by Bampton. He had been in the act of lighting his cigarette, but he allowed the match to burn down nearly to his fingers and then dropped it with a muttered exclamation in the fire. Finally:

"I don't know how you found out," he said, "but you evidently know the truth. Provided you assure me that you are not out to make a silly-season newspaper story, I'll tell you all I know."

Holmes laid his card on the table.

"Unless the ends of justice demand it," he said, "I give you my word that anything you care to say will go no further. You may speak freely before my friend, Dr. Watson. Simply tell me in as few words as possible what led you to court arrest in that manner."

"Right," replied Bampton, "I will." He half closed his eyes, reflectively. "I was having tea in the Lyons' Café, to which I always go, last Monday afternoon about four o'clock, when a man sat down facing me and got into conversation."

"Describe him!"

"He was a man rather above medium height. I should say about my own build; dark, going gray. He had a neat moustache and a short beard, and the look of a man who had travelled a lot. His skin was very tanned, almost as deeply as a tropical native. Not at all the sort of chap that goes in there as a rule. After a while, he made an extraordinary proposal. At first I thought he was joking, then when I grasped the idea that he was serious, I concluded he was mad. He asked me how much a year I earned, and I told him that Peters and Peters paid me 150 pounds. He said: 'I'll give you a year's salary to knock a man's hat off!'"

As Bampton spoke the words, he glanced at us with twinkling eyes; but although for my own part I was merely amused, Holmes's expression had grown very stern.

"Of course, I laughed," continued Bampton, "but when the man drew out a fat wallet and counted ten five-pound notes on the table, I began to think seriously about his proposal. Even supposing he was cracked, it was absolutely money for nothing.

"'Of course,' he said, 'you'll lose your job and you may be arrested, but you'll say that you had been out with a few friends and were a little excited, also that you never could stand white hats. Stick to that story and the balance of a hundred pounds will reach you on the following morning.'

"I asked him for further particulars, and I asked him why he had picked me for the job. He replied that he had been looking for some time for the right man; a man who was strong enough physically to accomplish the thing, and someone" — Bampton's eyes twinkled again — "with a dash of the devil in him, but at the same time a man who could be relied upon to stick to his guns and not to give the game away.

"You asked me to be brief, and I'll try to be. The man in the white hat was described to me, and the exact time and place of the meeting. I just had to grab his white hat, smash it, and face the music. I agreed. I don't deny that I had a couple of stiff drinks before I set out, but the memory of that fifty pounds locked up here in my room and the further hundred promised, bucked me up wonderfully. It was impossible to mistake my man; I could see him coming toward me as I waited just outside a sort of little restaurant called the Café Dame. As arranged, I bumped into him, grabbed his hat, and jumped on it."

He paused, raising his hand to his head reminiscently.

"My man was a bit of a scrapper," he continued, "and he played hell. I've never heard such language in my life, and the way he laid about me with his cane is something I am not likely to forget in a hurry. A crowd gathered, naturally, and (also naturally) I was 'pinched.' That didn't matter much. I got off lightly; and although I've been dismissed by Peters and Peters, twenty crisp fivers are locked in my trunk there, with the ten which I received in the City."

Holmes checked him.

"May I see the envelope in which they arrived?" he asked.

"Sorry," replied Bampton, "but I burned it. I thought it was playing the game to do so. It wouldn't have helped you much, though," he added; "It was an ordinary common envelope, posted in the City, address typewritten, and not a line enclosed."

"Registered?"

"No."

Bampton stood looking at us with a curious expression on his face, and then suddenly:

"There's one point," he said, "on which my conscience isn't easy. You know about that poor devil who fell out of a window? Well, it would never have happened if I hadn't kicked up a row in the street. There's no doubt he was leaning out to see what the disturbance was about when the accident occurred."

"Did you actually see him fall?" asked Holmes.

"No. He fell from a window several yards behind me in the side street, but I heard him cry out; and as I was lugged off by the police, I heard the bell of the ambulance which came to fetch him."

He paused again and stood rubbing his head ruefully.

"H'm," said Holmes; "was there anything particularly remarkable about this man in the Lyons' Café?"

Bampton reflected silently for some moments, and then:

"Nothing much," he confessed. "He was evidently a gentleman, wore a blue top-coat, a dark tweed suit, and what looked like a regimental tie, but I didn't see much of the colours. He was very tanned, as I have said, even to the backs of his hands — and *oh, yes!* there was one point: He had a gold-covered tooth."

"Which tooth?"

"I can't remember, except that it was on the left side, and I always noticed it when he smiled."

"Did he wear any ring or pin which you would recognize?"

"No."

"Had he any oddity of speech or voice?"

"No. Just a heavy, drawling manner. He spoke like thousands of other cultured Englishmen. But wait a minute — yes! There was one other point. Now I come to think of it, his eyes very slightly slanted upward."

Holmes stared.

"Like a Chinaman's?"

"Oh, nothing like that. Not so pronounced."

Holmes nodded briskly and buttoned up his overcoat.

"Thanks, Mr. Bampton," he said; "we will detain you no longer!"

As we descended the stairs, where the smell of frying sausages had given place to that of something burning — probably the sausages:

"I was half inclined to think that Major Ragstaff's ideas were traceable to a former touch of the sun," said Holmes. "I begin to believe that he has put us on the track of a highly unusual crime. I am sorry to delay dinner, Watson, but I propose to call at the Café Dame."

III.

A CRIMINAL GENIUS

On entering the doorway of the Café Dame, we found ourselves in a narrow passage. In front of us was a carpeted stair, and to the right a glass-panelled door communicating with a discreetly lighted little dining room which seemed to be well patronized. Opening the door Holmes beckoned to a waiter.

"I wish to see the proprietor," he said.

"Mr. Meyer is engaged at the moment, sir," was the reply.

"Where is he?"

"In his office upstairs, sir. He will be down in a moment."

The waiter hurried away, and Holmes stood glancing up the stairs as if in doubt what to do.

"I cannot imagine how such a place can pay," he muttered. "The rent must be enormous in this district."

But even before he ceased speaking, I became aware of an excited conversation which was taking place in some apartment above.

"It's scandalous!" I heard, in a woman's shrill voice. "You have no right to keep it! It's not your property, and I'm here to demand that you give it up."

A man's voice replied in voluble broken English, but I could only distinguish a word here and there. I saw that Holmes was interested, for catching my questioning glance, he raised his finger to his lips enjoining me to be silent.

"Oh, that's the game, is it?" continued the female voice. "Of course you know it's blackmail?"

A flow of unintelligible words answered this speech, then:

"I shall come back with someone," cried the invisible woman, "who will make you give it up!"

"Watson," whispered Holmes in my ear, "when that woman comes down, follow her! I'm afraid you will bungle the business, and I would not ask you to attempt it if big things were not at stake. Return here; I shall wait."

As a matter of fact, his sudden request had positively astounded me, but ere I had time for any reply, a door suddenly banged open above and a respectable-looking woman, who might have been some kind of upper servant, came quickly down the stairs. An expression of intense indignation rested upon her face, and without seeming to notice our presence, she brushed past us and went out into the street.

"Off you go, Watson!" said Holmes.

Seeing myself committed to an unpleasant business, I slipped out of the doorway and detected the woman five or six yards away hurrying in the direction of Piccadilly. I had no difficulty in following her, for she was evidently unsuspicious of my presence, and when presently she mounted a westward-bound 'bus I did likewise, but while she got inside I went on top, and occupied a seat on the near side whence I could observe anyone leaving the vehicle.

If I had not known Sherlock Holmes so well, I should have counted the whole business a ridiculous farce; but recognizing that something underlay these seemingly trivial and disconnected episodes, I lighted a cigarette and resigned myself to circumstance.

At Hyde Park Corner I saw the woman descending, and when presently she walked up Hamilton Place, I was not far behind her. At the door of an imposing mansion she stopped, and in response to a ring of the bell, the door was opened by a footman, and the woman hurried in. Evidently she was an inmate of the establishment; and conceiving that my duty was done when I had noted the number of the house, I retraced my steps to the corner; and, hailing a hansom, returned to the Café Dame.

On inquiring of the same waiter whom Holmes had accosted whether my friend was there:

"I think a gentleman is upstairs with Mr. Meyer," said the man.

"In his office?"

"Yes, sir."

Thereupon I mounted the stairs and before a half-open door paused. Holmes's voice was audible within, and therefore I knocked and entered.

I discovered Holmes standing by an American desk. Beside him in a revolving chair which, with the desk, constituted the principal furniture of a tiny office, sat a man in a dress-suit which had palpably not been made for him. He had a sullen and suspiciously Teutonic cast of countenance, and he was engaged in a voluble but hardly intelligible speech as I entered.

"Ha, Watson!" said Holmes, glancing over his shoulder, "did you manage?"

"Yes," I replied.

Holmes nodded shortly and turned again to the man in the chair.

"I am sorry to give you so much trouble, Mr. Meyer," he said, "but I should like my friend here to see the room above."

At this moment my attention was attracted by a singular object which lay upon the desk amongst a litter of bills and accounts. It was a piece of rusty iron bar somewhat less than three feet in length, and which once had been painted green.

"You are looking at this tragic fragment, Watson," said Holmes, taking up the bar. "Of course" — he shrugged his shoulders — "it explains the whole unfortunate occurrence. You see there was a flaw in the metal at this end, here" — he indicated the spot — "and the other end had evidently worn loose in its socket."

"But I don't understand."

"It will all be made clear at the inquest, no doubt. A most unfortunate thing for you, Mr. Meyer."

"Most unfortunate," declared the proprietor of the restaurant, extending his thick hands pathetically. "Most ruinous to my business."

"We will go upstairs now," said Holmes. "You will kindly lead the way, Mr. Meyer, and the whole thing will be quite clear to you, Watson."

As the proprietor walked out of the office and upstairs to the second floor Holmes whispered in my ear:

"Where did she go?"

"No. 13 Hamilton Place," I replied in an undertone.

"Good God!" muttered my friend, and clutched my arm so tightly that I winced. "Good God! The master touch, Watson! This crime was the work of a genius — of a genius with slightly, very slightly, oblique eyes."

Opening a door on the second landing, Mr. Meyer admitted us to a small supper-room. Its furniture consisted of a round dining table, several chairs, a couch, and very little else. I observed, however, that the furniture, carpet, and a few other appointments were of a character much more elegant than those of the public room below. A window which overlooked the street was open, so that the plush curtains which had been drawn aside moved slightly to and fro in the draught.

"The window of the tragedy, Watson," explained Holmes.

He crossed the room.

"If you will stand here beside me, you will see the gap in the railing caused by the breaking away of the fragment which now lies on Mr. Meyer's desk. Some few yards to the left in the street below is where the assault took place, of which we have heard, and the unfortunate Mr. De Lana, who was dining here alone — an eccentric custom of his — naturally ran to the window upon hearing the disturbance and leaned out, supporting his weight upon the railing. The rail collapsed, and — we know the rest."

"It will ruin me," groaned Meyer; "it will give bad repute to my establishment."

"I fear it will," agreed Holmes sympathetically, "unless we can manage to clear up one or two little difficulties which I have observed. For instance" — he tapped the proprietor on the shoulder confidentially — "have you any idea, any hazy idea, of the identity of the woman who was dining here with Mr. De Lana on Wednesday night?"

The effect of this simple inquiry upon the proprietor was phenomenal. His fat pallid face assumed a sort of leaden hue, and his already prominent eyes protruded abnormally. He licked his lips.

"I tell you — already I tell you," he muttered, "that Mr. De Lana, he engage this room every Wednesday and sometimes also Friday, and dine here by himself."

"And I tell you," said Holmes sweetly, "that you are an inspired liar. You smuggled her out by the side entrance after the accident."

"The side entrance?" muttered Meyer. "The side entrance?"

"Exactly; the side entrance. There is something else which I must ask you to tell me. Who had engaged this room on Tuesday night, the night before the accident?"

The proprietor's expression remained uncomprehending.

"A gentleman," he said. "I never see him before."

"Another solitary diner?" suggested Holmes.

"Yes, he is alone all the evening waiting for a friend who does not arrive."

"Ah," mused Holmes — "alone all the evening, was he? And his friend disappointed him. May I suggest that he was a dark man? Gray at the temples, having a dark beard and moustache, and a very tanned face? His eyes slanted slightly upward?"

"Yes! yes!" cried Meyer, and his astonishment was patently unfeigned. "It is a friend of yours?"

"A friend of mine, yes," said Holmes absently, but his expression was very grim. "What time did he finally leave?"

"He waited until after eleven o'clock. The dinner is spoilt. He pays, but does not complain."

"No," said Holmes musingly, "he had nothing to complain about. One more question, my friend. When the lady escaped hurriedly on Wednesday night, what was it that she left behind and what price are you trying to extort from her for returning it?"

At that the man collapsed entirely.

"Ah, Gott!" he cried, and raised his hand to his clammy forehead. "You will ruin me. I am a ruined man. I don't try to extort anything. I run an honest business — "

"And one of the most profitable in the world," added Holmes, "since the days of Thais to our own. Even at Bond Street rentals I assume that a house of assignation is a golden enterprise."

"Ah!" groaned Meyer, "I am ruined, so what does it matter? I tell you everything. I know Mr. De Lana who engages my room regularly, but I don't know who the lady is who meets him here. No! I swear it! But always it is the same lady. When he falls, I am downstairs in my office, and I hear him cry out. The lady comes running from the room and begs of me to get her away without being seen and to keep all mention of her out of the matter."

"What did she pay you?" asked Holmes.

"Pay me?" muttered Meyer, pulled up thus shortly in the midst of his statement.

"Pay you. Exactly. Don't argue; answer."

The man delivered himself of a guttural, choking sound, and finally:

"She promised one hundred pounds," he confessed hoarsely.

"But you surely did not accept a mere promise? Out with it. What did she give you?"

"A ring," came the confession at last.

"A ring. I see. I will take it with me if you don't mind. And now, finally, what was it that she left behind?"

"Ah, Gott!" moaned the man, dropping into a chair and resting his arms upon the table. "It is all a great panic, you see. I hurry her out by the back stair from this landing and she forgets her bag."

"Her bag? Good."

"Then I clear away the remains of dinner so I can say Mr. De Lana is dining alone. It is as much my interest as the lady's."

"Of course! I quite understand. I will trouble you no more, Mr. Meyer, except to step into your office and to relieve you of that incriminating evidence, the lady's bag, and her ring."

IV.

THE ORIENTAL EYES

"Do you understand, Watson?" said Holmes as the hansom bore us toward Hamilton Place. "Do you grasp the details of this cunning scheme?"

"On the contrary," I replied, "I am hopelessly at sea."

Nevertheless, I had forgotten that I was hungry in the excitement which now claimed me. For although the thread upon which these seemingly disconnected things hung was invisible to me, I recognized that Bampton, the city clerk, the bearded stranger who had made so singular a proposition to him, the white-hatted major, the dead stockbroker, and the mysterious woman whose presence in the case the clear sight of Holmes had promptly detected, all were linked together by some subtle chain. I was convinced, too, that my friend held at least one end of that chain in his grip.

"In order to prepare your mind for the interview which I hope to obtain this evening," continued Holmes, "let me enlighten you upon one or two points which may seem obscure. In the first place, you recognize that anyone leaning out of the window on the second floor would almost automatically rest his weight upon the iron bar which was placed there for that very purpose, since the ledge is unusually low?"

"Quite," I replied, "and it also follows that if the bar gave way, anyone thus leaning on it would be pitched into the street."

"Your reasoning is correct."

"But, my dear fellow," said I, "how could such an accident have been foreseen?"

"You speak of an accident. This was no accident! One end of the bar had been filed completely through, although the file marks had been carefully concealed with rust and dirt; and the other end had been wrenched out from its socket and then replaced in such a way that anyone leaning upon the bar could not fail to be precipitated into the street!"

"Good heavens! Then you mean — "

"I mean, Watson, that the man who occupied the supper room on the night before the tragedy — the dark man, tanned and bearded, with slightly oblique eyes — spent his time in filing through that bar — in short, in preparing a death trap!"

I was almost dumbfounded.

"But, Holmes," I said, "assuming that he knew his victim would be the next occupant of the room, how could he know — ?"

I stopped. Suddenly, as if a curtain had been raised, the details of what I now perceived to be a fiendishly cunning murder were revealed to me.

"According to his own account, Watson," resumed Holmes, "Major Ragstaff regularly passed along that street with military punctuality at the same hour every night. You may take it for granted that the murderer was well aware of this. As a matter of fact, I happen to know that he was. We must also take it for granted that the murderer knew of these little dinners for two which took place in the private room above the Café Dame every Wednesday — and sometimes on Friday. Around the figure of the methodical major — with his conspicuous white hat as a sort of focus — was built up one of the most ingenious schemes of murder with which I have ever come in contact. The victim literally killed himself."

"But, Holmes, the victim might have ignored the disturbance."

"That is where I first detected the touch of genius, Watson. He recognized the voice of one of the combatants — or his companion did. Here we are."

The hansom drew up before the house in Hamilton Place. We alighted, and Holmes pressed the bell. The same footman whom I had seen admit the woman opened the door.

"Is Lady Ireton at home?" asked Holmes.

As he uttered the name I literally held my breath. We had come to the house of Major Ragstaff's daughter, the Marchioness of Ireton, one of society's most celebrated and beautiful hostesses! — the wife of a peer famed alike as sportsman, soldier, and scholar.

"I believe she is dining at home, sir," said the man. "Shall I inquire?"

"Be good enough to do so," replied Holmes, and gave him a card. "Inform her that I wish to return to her a handbag which she lost a few days ago."

The man ushered us into an anteroom opening off the lofty and rather gloomy hall, and as the door closed:

"Holmes," I said in a stage whisper, "am I to believe — "

"Can you doubt it?" returned Holmes with a grim smile.

A few moments later we were shown into a charmingly intimate little boudoir in which Lady Ireton was waiting to receive us. She was a strikingly handsome brunette, but to-night her face, which normally, I think, possessed rich colouring, was almost pale, and there was a hunted look in her dark eyes which made me wish to be anywhere rather than where I found myself. Without preamble she rose and addressed Holmes:

"I fail to understand your message, sir," she said, and I admired the imperious courage with which she faced him. "You say you have recovered a handbag which I had lost?"

Holmes bowed, and from the pocket of his greatcoat took out a silken-tasselled bag.

"The one which you left in the Café Dame, Lady Ireton," he replied. "Here also I have" — from another pocket he drew out a diamond ring — "something which was extorted from you by that fellow Meyer."

Without touching her recovered property, Lady Ireton sank slowly down into the chair from which she had arisen, her gaze fixed as if hypnotically upon the speaker.

"My friend, Dr. Watson, is aware of all the circumstances," continued the latter, "but he is as anxious as I am to terminate this painful interview. I surmise that what occurred on Wednesday night was this — (correct me if I am wrong): While dining with Mr. De Lana you heard sounds of altercation in the street below. May I suggest that you recognized one of the voices?"

Lady Ireton, still staring straight before her at Holmes, inclined her head in assent.

"I heard my father's voice," she said hoarsely.

"Quite so," he continued. "I am aware that Major Ragstaff is your father." He turned to me: "Do you recognize the touch of genius at last?"

Then, again addressing Lady Ireton: "You naturally suggested to your companion that he should look out of the window in order to learn what was taking place. The next thing you knew was that he had fallen into the street below?"

Lady Ireton shuddered and raised her hands to her face.

"It is retribution," she whispered. "I have brought this ruin upon myself. But he does not deserve — "

Her voice faded into silence.

"You refer to your husband, Lord Ireton?" said Holmes.

Lady Ireton nodded, and again recovering power of speech:

"It was to have been our last meeting," she said, looking up at Holmes.

She shuddered, and her eyes blazed into sudden fierceness. Then, clenching her hands, she looked aside.

"Oh, God, the shame of this hour!" she whispered.

And I would have given much to have been spared the spectacle of this proud, erring woman's humiliation. But Sherlock Holmes was scientifically remorseless. I could detect no pity in his glance.

"I would give my life willingly to spare my husband the knowledge of what has been," said Lady Ireton in a low, monotonous voice. "Three times I sent my maid to Meyer to recover my bag, but he demanded a price which even I could not pay. Now it is all discovered, and Harry will know."

"That, I fear, is unavoidable, Lady Ireton," declared Holmes. "May I ask where Lord Ireton is at present?"

"He is in Africa after big game."

"H'm," said Holmes, "in Africa, and after big game? I can offer you one consolation, Lady Ireton. In his own interests Meyer will stick to his first assertion that Mr. De Lana was dining alone."

A strange, horribly pathetic look came into the woman's haunted eyes.

"You — you — are not acting for — ?" she began.

"I am acting for no one," replied Holmes tersely. "Upon my friend's discretion you may rely as upon my own."

"Then why should he ever know?" she whispered.

"Why, indeed," murmured Holmes, "since he is in Africa?"

As we descended the stair to the hall my friend paused and pointed to a life-sized oil painting by London's most fashionable portrait painter. It was that of a man in the uniform of a Guards officer, a dark man, slightly gray at the temples, his face very tanned as if by exposure to the sun.

"Having had no occasion for disguise when the portrait was painted," said Holmes, "Lord Ireton appears here without the beard; and as he is not represented smiling one cannot see the gold tooth. But the painter, if anything, has accentuated the slanted eyes. You see, the fourth marquis — the present Lord Ireton's father — married one of the world-famous Yen Sun girls, daughters of the mandarin of that name by an Irish wife. Hence, the eyes. And hence — "

"But, Holmes — it was murder!"

"Not within the meaning of the law, Watson. It was a recrudescence of Chinese humour! Lord Ireton is officially in Africa (and he went actually after 'big game'). The counsel is not born who could secure a conviction. We are somewhat late, but shall therefore have less difficulty in finding a table at Prince's."

The Affair of the Barber Atrocity

I.

A STRANGE DISAPPEARANCE

"Pull that light lower," ordered Inspector Lestrade of Scotland Yard. "There you are, Mr. Holmes; what do you make of it?"

Sherlock Holmes and I gingerly bent over to view the ghastly exhibit to which the police official had drawn our attention, and for which purpose we had journeyed from Holmes' lodgings in Baker Street to Wapping Police Station.

It was the body of a man dressed solely in ragged shirt and trousers. But the remarkable feature of his appearance lay in the fact that every scrap of hair from chin, lip, eyebrows, and skull had been shaved off!

There was another facial disfigurement, peculiarly horrible, which my pen may not describe.

"Impossible to identify!" murmured Holmes. "Yes, you were right, Inspector; this is certainly a victim of Oriental deviltry. Look here, Watson!"

He indicated three small wounds, one situated on the left shoulder and the others on the forearm of the dead man.

"The divisional surgeon cannot account for them," said Lestrade. "They are quite superficial, and he thinks they may be due to the fact that the body got entangled with something in the river."

"They are due to the fact that the man had a birthmark on his shoulder and something — probably a name or some device — tattooed on his arm," said Holmes quietly. "Some few years ago, I met with a similar case in Istanbul. A woman," he added, significantly.

Detective-Inspector Lestrade listened to my companion with respect, for apart from his established reputation as a consulting detective which had made his name familiar in nearly every capital of the civilized world, Sherlock Holmes' work in Constantinople during the six months preceding war with Turkey had merited higher reward than it had ever received. Had his recommendations been adopted, the course of history must have been materially changed.

"You think it's a Chinatown case, then, Mr. Holmes?"

"Possibly," was the guarded answer.

Sherlock Holmes nodded to the constable in charge, and the ghastly figure was promptly covered up again. My friend stood staring vacantly at Lestrade, and presently:

"The chief actor, I think, will prove to be not Chinese," he said, turned, and walked out.

"If there's any development," remarked Lestrade as the three of us entered Holmes's carriage, which stood at the door, "I will, of course, report to you, Mr. Holmes. But in the absence of any clue or mark of identification, I fear the verdict will be, 'Body of a man unknown,' etc., which has marked the finish of a good many in this cheerful quarter of London."

"Quite so," said Holmes, absently. "It presents extraordinary features, though, and may not end as you suppose. However — where do you want me to drop you, Lestrade — at the Yard?"

"Oh no," answered Lestrade. "I made a special visit to Wapping just to get your opinion on the shaven man. I'm really going down to Deepbrow to look into that new disappearance case; the daughter of the gamekeeper. You'll have read of it?"

"I have," said Holmes shortly.

Indeed, readers of the daily press were growing tired of seeing on the contents bills:

"Another girl missing." The circumstance (which might have been no more than coincidence) that three girls had disappeared within the last eight weeks leaving no trace behind, had stimulated the professional scribes to link the cases, although no visible link had been found, and to enliven a somewhat dull journalistic season with theories about "a new Ripper menace."

The vanishing of this fourth girl had inspired them to some startling headlines, and the case had interested me personally for the reason that I was acquainted with Sir Howard Hepwell, one of whose gamekeepers was the stepfather of the missing Molly Clayton. Moreover, it was hinted that she had gone away in the company of Captain Ronald Vane, at that time a guest of Sir Howard's at the Manor.

In fact, Sir Howard had sent me a cable asking me if I could induce Holmes to run down, but my friend had expressed himself as disinterested in a common case of elopement. Now, as Lestrade spoke, I glanced aside at Holmes, wondering if the fact that so celebrated a member of the C.I.D. as Detective-Inspector Lestrade had been put in charge would induce him to change his mind.

We were traversing a particularly noisy and unsavoury section of the Commercial Road, and although I could see that Lestrade was anxious to impart particulars of the case to Holmes, so loud was the din that I recognized the impossibility of conversing, and therefore:

"Have you time to call at my rooms, Lestrade?" I asked.

"Well," he replied, "I have three-quarters of an hour."

"You can do it in the carriage," said Holmes suddenly. "I have been asked to look into this case myself, and before I definitely decline I should like to hear your version of the matter."

Accordingly, we three presently gathered in my chambers, and Lestrade, with one eye on the clock, outlined the few facts at that time in his possession respecting the missing girl.

Two days before the news of the disappearance had been published broadcast under such headings as I have already indicated, a significant scene had been enacted in the gamekeeper's cottage.
Molly Clayton, a girl whose remarkable beauty had made her a central figure in numerous scandalous stories, for such is the charity of rural neighbours, was detected by her

stepfather, about eight in the evening, slipping out of the cottage.

"Where be ye goin', hussy?" he demanded, grasping her promptly by the arm.

"For a walk!" she replied defiantly.

"A walk wi' that fine soger from t' Manor!" roared Bramber furiously. "You'll be sorry yet, you barefaced gadabout! Must I tell you again that t' man's a villain?"

The girl wrenched her arm from Bramber's grasp, and blazed defiance from her beautiful eyes.

"He knows how to respect a woman — what you don't!" she retorted hotly.

"So I don't respect you, my angel?" shouted her stepfather. "Then you know what you can do! The door's open and there's few'll miss you!"

Snatching her hat, the girl, very white, made to go out. Whereat the gamekeeper, a brutal man with small love for Molly, and maddened by her taking him at his word, seized her suddenly by her abundant fair hair and hauled her back into the room.

A violent scene followed, at the end of which Molly fainted and Bramber came out and locked the door.

When he came back about half-past nine the girl was missing. She did not reappear that night, and the police were advised in the morning. Their most significant discovery was this:

Captain Ronald Vane, on the night of Molly's disappearance, had left the Manor House, after dining alone with his host, Sir Howard Hepwell, saying that he proposed to take a stroll as far as the Deep Wood.

He never returned!

From the moment that Gamekeeper Bramber left his cottage, and the moment when Sir Howard Hepwell parted from his guest after dinner, the world to which these two people, Molly Clayton and Captain Vane, were known, knew them no more!

I was about to say that they were never seen again. But to me has fallen the task of relating how and where Sherlock Holmes and I met with Captain Vane and Molly Clayton.

At the end of the Inspector's account:

"H'm," said Holmes, glancing under his thick brows in my direction, "could you spare the time, Watson?"

"To go to Deepbrow?" I asked with interest.

"Yes; we have ten minutes to catch the train."

"I'll come," said I. "Sir Howard will be delighted to see you, Holmes."

II.

THE CLUE OF THE PHOTOGRAPHS

"What do you make of it, Inspector?" asked my friend. Detective-Inspector Lestrade smiled, and scratched his chin.

"There was no need for me to come down!" he replied. "And certainly no need for you, Mr. Holmes!"

Holmes bowed, smiling, at the implied compliment.

"It's a common or garden elopement!" continued the detective. "Vane's reputation is absolutely rotten, and the girl was clearly infatuated. He must have cared a good bit, too. He'll be cashiered, as sure as a gun!"

Leaving Sir Howard at the Manor, we had joined Inspector Lestrade at a spot where the baronet's preserves bordered a narrow lane. Here the ground was soft, and the detective drew Holmes's attention to a number of footprints by a stile.

"I've got evidence that he was seen here with the girl on other occasions. Now, Mr. Holmes, I'll ask you to look over these footprints."

Holmes dropped to his knees and made a brief but close examination of the ground round about. One particularly clear imprint of a pointed toe he noticed especially; and Lestrade, diving into the pocket of his light overcoat, produced a patent-leather shoe, such as is used for evening wear.

"He had a spare pair in his bag," he explained nonchalantly, "and his man did not prove incorruptible!"

Holmes took the shoe and placed it in the impression. It fitted perfectly!

"This is Molly Clayton, I take it?" he said, indicating the prints of a woman's foot.

"Yes," assented Lestrade. "You'll notice that they stood for some little time and then walked off, very close together."

Holmes nodded absently.

"We lose them along here," continued Lestrade, leading up the lane; "but at the corner by the big haystack they join up with the tracks of a Phaeton! I ask for nothing clearer! There was rain that afternoon, but there's been none since."

"What does the Captain's man think?"

"The same as I do! He's not surprised at any madness on Vane's part, with a pretty woman in the case!"

"The girl left nothing behind — no note?"

"Nothing."

"Traced the carriage?"

"No. It must have been hired or borrowed from a long distance off."

Where the tracks of the tires were visible we stopped, and Holmes made a careful examination of the marks.

"Seems to have had a struggle with her," he said, dryly.

"Very likely!" agreed Lestrade, without interest.

Holmes crawled about on the ground for some time, to the great detriment of his Harris tweeds, but finally arose, a curious expression on his face — which, however, the detective evidently failed to observe.

We returned to the Manor House where Sir Howard was awaiting us, his good-humoured red face more red than usual; and in the library, with its sporting prints and its works for the most part dealing with riding, hunting, racing, and golf (except for a sprinkling of Nat Gould's novels and some examples of the older workmanship of Whyte-Melville), we were presently comfortably ensconced. On a side table were placed a generous supply of liquid refreshments, cigars, and cigarettes; so that we made ourselves quite comfortable, and Sir Howard restrained his indignation, until each had a glass before him and all were smoking.

"Now," he began, "what have you got to report, gentlemen? You, Inspector," he pointed with his cigar toward Lestrade, "have seen Vane's man and all of you have been down to look at these demmed tracks. I only want to hear one thing; that you expect to trace the disgraceful couple. I'll see to it" — his voice rose almost to a shout — " that Vane is kicked out of the service, and as to that shameless brat of Bramber's, I wish her no worse than the blackguard's company!"

"One moment, Sir Howard, one moment," said Holmes quietly; "there are always two sides to a case."

"What do you mean, Mr. Holmes? There's only one side that interests me — the outrage inflicted upon my hospitality by this dirty guest of mine. For the girl I don't give tuppence; she was bound to come to a bad end."

"Well," said Holmes, "before we pronounce the final verdict upon either of them I should like to interview Bramber. Perhaps," he added, turning to Lestrade, "it would be as well if Dr. Watson and I went alone. The presence of an official detective sometimes awes this class of witness."

"Quite right, quite right!" agreed Sir Howard, waving his cigar vigorously. "Go and see Bramber, Mr. Holmes; tell him that no blame attaches to himself whatever; also, tell him with my compliments that his stepdaughter is — "

"Quite so, quite so," interrupted Holmes, endeavouring to hide a smile. "I understand your feelings, Sir Howard, but again I ask you to reserve your verdict until all the facts are before us."

As a result, Holmes and I presently set out for the gamekeeper's cottage, and as the man had been warned that we should visit him, he was on the porch smoking his pipe. A big, dark, ugly fellow he proved to be, of a very forbidding cast of countenance. Having introduced ourselves:

"I always knowed she'd come to a bad end!" declared Gamekeeper Bramber, almost echoing Sir Howard's words. "One o' these gentlemen o' hers was sure to be the finish of her!"

"She had other admirers — before Captain Vane?"

"Aye! the hussy! There was a black-faced villain not six months since! He got t' vain cat to go to London an' have her photograph done in a dress any decent woman would 'a' blushed to look at! Like one o' these Venuses up at t' Manor! Good riddance! She took after her mother!"

The violent old ruffian was awkward to examine, but Holmes persevered.

"This previous admirer caused her to be photographed in that way, did he? Have you a copy?"

"No!" blazed Bramber. "What I found I burnt! He ran off, like I told her he would — an' her cryin' her eyes out! But the pretty soger dried her tears quick enough!"

"Do you know this man's name?"

"No. A foreigner, he was."

"Where were the photographs done — in London, you say?"

"Aye."

"Do you know by what photographer?"

"I don't! An' I don't care! Piccadilly they had on 'em, which was good enough for me."

"Have you her picture?"

"No!"

"Did she receive a letter on the day of her disappearance?"

"Maybe."

"Good day!" said Holmes. "And let me add that the atmosphere of her home was hardly conducive to ideal conduct!"

Leaving Bramber to digest this rebuke, we came out of the cottage. Dusk was falling now, and by the time that we regained the Manor the place was lighted up. Inspector Lestrade was waiting for us in the library.

"Well?" he said, smiling slightly as we entered.

"Nothing much," replied Holmes dryly, "except that I don't wonder at the girl's leaving such a home."

"What's that! What!" roared a big voice, and Sir Howard came into the room. "I tell you, Bramber only had one fault as a stepfather; he wasn't heavy-handed enough. A bad lot, sir, a bad lot!"

"Well, sir," said Inspector Lestrade, looking from one to another, "personally, beyond the usual inquiries at railway stations, etc., I cannot see that we can do much here. Don't you agree with me, Mr. Holmes?"

Holmes nodded.

"Quite," he replied. "There is a late train to town which I think we could catch if we started at once."

"Eh?" roared Sir Howard; "you're not going back to-night? Your rooms are ready for you, dash it!"

"I quite appreciate the kindness, Sir Howard," replied Holmes; "but I have urgent business to attend to in London. Believe me, my departure is unavoidable."

The blue eyes of the baronet gleamed with the simple cunning of his kind.

"You've got something up your sleeve," he roared. "I know you have, I know you have!"

Inspector Lestrade looked at me significantly, but I could only shrug my shoulders in reply; for in these moods Holmes was as inscrutable as the Sphinx.

However, he had his way, and Sir Howard hurriedly putting a carriage in commission, we raced for the local station and just succeeded in picking up the express at Claybury.

Lestrade was rather silent throughout the journey, often glancing in my friend's direction, but Holmes made no further reference to the case beyond outlining the interview with Bramber, until, as we were parting at the London terminus, Lestrade to report to Scotland Yard and I to go to Holmes's rooms:

"How long do you think it will take you to find that photographer, Lestrade?" he asked. "Piccadilly is a sufficient clue."

"Well," replied the Inspector, "nothing can be done to-night, of course, but I should think by mid-day tomorrow the matter should be settled."

"Right," said Holmes shortly. "May I ask you to report the result to me, Lestrade?"

"I will report without fail."

III.

PROFESSOR MORIARTY

It was not until the evening of the following day that Holmes rang me up.

"I want you to come round at once," he said urgently. "The Deepbrow case is developing along lines which I confess I had anticipated, but which are dramatic nevertheless."

Knowing that Holmes did not lightly make such an assertion, I put aside the work upon which I was engaged and hurried around to Baker Street. I found my friend, pipe in mouth, walking up and down his smoke-laden study in a state which I knew to betoken suppressed excitement.

"Did Lestrade find your photographer?" I asked on entering.

"Yes," he replied. "A first-class man, as I had anticipated. As I had further anticipated he did a number of copies of the picture for the foreign gentleman — about fifty, in fact!"

"Fifty!"

"Yes! Does the significance of that fact strike you?" asked Holmes, a queer smile stealing across his tanned, clean-shaven face.

"It is an extraordinary thing for even an ardent admirer to have so many reproductions done of the same picture!"

"It is! I will show you now what I found trodden into one of the footprints where the struggle took place beside the carriage."

Holmes produced a piece of thick silk twine.

"What is it?"

"It is a link, Watson — a link to seek which I really went down to Deepbrow." He stared at me quizzically, but my answering look must have been a blank one. "It is part of the tassel of one of those red cloth caps commonly called in England, a fez!"

He continued to stare at me and I to stare at the piece of silk; then:

"What is the next move?" I demanded. "Your new clue rather bewilders me."

"The next move," he said, "is to retire to the adjoining room and make ourselves look as much like a couple of Oriental commercial travellers as our correctly British appearance will allow!"

"What!" I cried.

"That's it!" laughed Holmes. "I have a perpetual tan, and I think I can give you a temporary one which I keep in a bottle for the purpose."

Twenty minutes later, then, having quitted Holmes's chambers by a back way opening into one of those old-world courts which abound in this part of the metropolis, two quietly attired Eastern gentlemen got into a hansom at the corner of Baker Street and proceeded in the direction of Limehouse.

There are haunts in many parts of London whose very existence is unsuspected by all but the few; haunts unvisited by the tourist and even unknown to the copy-hunting pressman. Into a quiet thoroughfare not three minutes' walk from the busy life of West India Dock Road, Holmes led the way. Before a door sandwiched in between the entrance to a Greek tobacconist's establishment and a boarded shop-front, he paused and turned to me.

"Whatever you see or hear," he cautioned, "express no surprise. Above all, show no curiosity."

He rang the bell beside the door, and almost immediately it was opened by a dark-visaged woman, grossly and repellently ugly.

Holmes pattered something in what sounded like Arabic, whereat the woman displayed the utmost servility, ushering us into an ill-lighted passage with every evidence of respect. Following this passage to its termination, an inner door was opened, and a burst of discordant music greeted us, together with a wave of tobacco smoke. We entered.

Despite my friend's particular injunctions to the contrary, I gave a start of amazement.

We stood in the doorway of a fairly large apartment having a divan round three of its sides. This divan was occupied by ten or a dozen men of mixed nationalities — Arabs, Greeks, Lascars, and others. They smoked cigarettes for the most part and sipped Mokha from little cups. A girl was performing a wriggling dance upon the square carpet occupying the centre of the floor, accompanied by a Nubian boy who twanged upon a guitar, and by most of the assembled company, who clapped their hands to the music or droned a low, tuneless dirge.

Shortly after our entrance the performance terminated, and the girl retired through a curtained doorway at the farther end of the room. Our presence being now observed, suspicious glances were cast in our direction, and a very aged man, who sat smoking a narghli near the door by which the girl had made her exit, gravely waved towards us the amber mouthpiece which he held in his hand.

Holmes walked straight across to him, I close at his heels. The light of a lamp which hung close by fell fully upon my friend's face; and, rising from his seat, the old man greeted him with the dignified and graceful salutation of the East. At his request we seated ourselves beside him, and, while we all three smoked excellent Turkish cigarettes, Holmes and he conversed in a low tone. Suddenly, at some remark of my friend's, our strange host rose to his feet, an angry frown contracting his heavy eyebrows.

Silence fell upon the company.

In a loud and peremptory voice he called out something in Arabic.

Instantly I detected a old man near the entrance door, and whom I had not hitherto observed, slipping furtively into the shadow, with a view, as I thought, to secret departure. He seemed to be deformed in some way and had the most evil, scar-marked face I had ever beheld in my life. "Stop — you'll not escape me this time! Holmes called to the old man. Whereupon, with a sort of animal snarl quite indescribable, the fellow drew out a long, wicked knife! Two men who had been on the point of seizing him fell back.

"Hold him!" shouted Holmes, springing forward — "hold him! *It's Professor Moriarty!* Take care. The knife is poisoned!"

But Holmes was too late. Turning, the strange and formidable-looking cripple ran like the wind! Ere hand could be raised to stay him, he was through the doorway!

"That settles it," said Holmes grimly, as once more I found myself in a hansom beside him. "I was right; he survived the fall at Reichenbach!"

"Can it truly be Moriarty?" I asked in bewilderment.

"I had heard of his villany in the Arab world, and I suspected. The worst monster in Europe, Asia, or Africa!" cried my companion. "I have wasted precious time to-day. I might have known."

He drummed irritably upon his knees. "The place we have just left is a sort of club, you understand, Watson, and Hakim is the proprietor or host as well as being an old gentleman of importance and authority in the Arab world. I told him of my suspicions — which step I should have taken earlier — and they were instantly confirmed. My man was there — recognized me — and bolted! He'll forestall us."

"But my dear fellow," I said patiently — "who is this man, and what has he to do with the Deepbrow case?"

"He is the blackest scoundrel breathing!" answered Holmes bitterly. "As to what he has to do with the case? At any rate, I know where to find him now — and we may not be too late after all."

"But what is he up to now?"

"He is Professor Moriarty! As to what he is doing — you will soon learn."

IV.

THE HOUSE BY THE RIVER

On quitting the singular Oriental club, Holmes had first raced off to a public telephone, where he had spoken for some time — as I now divined — to Scotland Yard. For when we presently arrived at the headquarters of the Metropolitan Police, I was surprised to find Inspector Lestrade awaiting us. Leaning out of the hansom window:

"Yes?" called Holmes excitedly. "Was I right?"

"You were, Mr. Holmes," answered Lestrade, who seemed to be no less excited than my companion. "I got the man's reply an hour ago."

"I knew it!" said Holmes shortly. "Get in, Lestrade; we haven't a minute to waste."

The Inspector joined us in the hansom, having first given instructions to the chauffeur. As we set out once more:

"You have had very little time to make the necessary arrangements," continued my friend.

"Time enough," replied Lestrade. "They will not be expecting us."

"I'm not so sure of it. The greatest criminal in the civilized world recognized me and then made good his escape three minutes before I called you up. However, there is at least a fighting chance."

Little more was said from that moment until the end of the drive, both my companions seeming to be consumed by an intense eagerness to reach our destination. At last the hansom drew up in a deserted street. I had rather lost my bearings; but I knew that we were once more somewhere in the Chinatown area.

"Follow us until we get into the house," Holmes said to Inspector Lestrade, "and wait out of sight. If you hear me blow this whistle, bring up the men you have posted — as quick as you like! But make it your particular business to see that no one gets out!"

Into a pitch-dark yard we turned, and I felt a shudder of apprehension upon observing that it was the entrance to a wharf. Dully gleaming in the moonlight, the Thames, that grave of many a ghastly secret, flowed beneath us. Emerging from the shadow of the archway, we paused before a door in the wall on our left.

At that moment something gleamed through the air, whizzed past my ear, and fell with a metallic jingle on the stones!

Instinctively we both looked up.

At an unlighted window on the first floor I caught a fleeting glimpse of a dark face.

"You were right!" I said. "Professor Moriarty has forestalled us!"

Holmes stooped and picked up a knife with a broad and very curious blade. He slipped it into his pocket, nonchalantly.

"All evidence!" he said. "Keep in the shadow and bend down. I am going to stand on your shoulders and get into that window!"

Wondering at his daring, I nevertheless obeyed; and Holmes succeeded, although not without difficulty, in achieving his purpose. A moment after he had disappeared in the blackness of the room above.

"Stand clear, Watson!" I heard.

Two of the cushion seats sometimes called "poof-ottomans" were thrown down.

"Up you come!" called Holmes. "I'll grasp your hands if you can reach."

It proved no easy task, but I finally managed to scramble up beside my friend — to find myself in a dark and stuffy little room.

"This way!" said Holmes rapidly — "upstairs."

He led the way without more ado, but it was with serious misgivings that I stumbled up a darkened stair in the rear of my greatly daring friend.

A pistol cracked in the darkness — and my fez was no longer on my head!

Holmes's pistol answered, and we stumbled through a heavily curtained door into a heated room, the air of which was laden with some Eastern perfume. In the dim light from a silken-shaded lantern a figure showed, momentarily, darting across the place before us.

Again Holmes's pistol spoke, but, as it seemed, ineffectively.

I had little enough opportunity to survey my surroundings; yet even in those brief, breathless moments I saw enough of the place wherein we stood to make me doubt the evidence of my senses! Outside, I knew, lay a dingy wharf, amid a maze of mean streets; here was an opulently furnished apartment with a strong Oriental note in the decorations!

Snatching an electric torch from his pocket, Holmes leaped through a doorway draped with rich Persian tapestry, and I came close on his heels. Outside was darkness. A strong draught met us; and, passing along a carpeted corridor, we never halted until we came to a room filled with the weirdest odds and ends, apparently collected from every quarter of the globe.

Crack!

A bullet flattened itself on the wall behind us!

"Good job he can't shoot straight!" rapped Holmes.

The ray of the torch suddenly picked out the head and shoulders of a man who was descending through a trap in the floor! Ere we had time to shoot he was gone! I saw his brown fingers relax their hold — and a bundle which he had evidently hoped to take with him was left lying upon the floor.

Together we ran to the trap and looked down.

Slowly moving tidal water flowed darkly beneath us! For twenty breathless seconds we watched — but nothing showed upon the surface.

"I hope his swimming is no better than his shooting," I said.

"It can avail him little," replied Holmes grimly; "a river-police boat is waiting for anyone who tries to escape from that side of the house. We are by no means alone in this affair, Watson. But, firstly, what have we here!" He took up the bundle which the fugitive had deserted. "Something incriminating when Professor Moriarty dared not stay to face it out! He would never have deserted this place in the ordinary way. That fellow who was such a bad shot was left behind, when the news of our approach reached here, to make a desperate attempt to remove some piece of evidence! I'll swear to it. But we were too soon for him!"

All the time he was busily removing the pieces of sacking and scraps of Oriental stuff with which the bundle was fastened; and finally he drew out a dress-suit, together with the linen, collar, shoes, and underwear — a complete outfit, in fact — and on top of the whole was a soft gray felt hat!

Eagerly Holmes searched the garments for some name of a maker by which their owner might be identified. Presently, inside the lining of the breast pocket, where such a mark is usually found, he discovered the label of a well-known West End firm.

"The police can confirm it, Watson!" he said, looking up, his face slightly flushed with triumph; "but I, personally, have no doubt!"

"You may have no doubt, Holmes," I retorted, "but I am full of doubt! What is the significance of this discovery to which you seem to attach so much importance?"

"At the moment," replied my friend, "never mind; I still have hopes — although they have grown somewhat slender — of making a much more important discovery."

"Why not permit the police to aid in the search?"

"The police are more useful in their present occupation," he replied. "We are dealing with the most cunning criminal mind produced by East or West, and I don't mean to let him slip through my fingers if he is in this house! Nevertheless, Watson, I am submitting you to rather an appalling risk, I know; for our man is desperate, and if he is still in the place will prove as dangerous as a cornered rat."

"But the man who dropped through the trap?"

"The man who dropped through the trap," said Holmes, "was not Professor Moriarty — and it is Professor Moriarty for whom I am looking!"

"You think he is still here?"

Holmes nodded, and having listened intently for a few moments, proceeded again to search the singular apartments of the abode. In each was evidence of Oriental occupancy; indeed, some of the rooms possessed a sort of Arabian Nights atmosphere. But no living creature was to be seen or heard anywhere. It was while the two of us, having examined every inch of wall, I should think, in the building, were standing staring rather blankly at each other in the room with the lighted lantern, that I saw Holmes's expression change.

"Why," he muttered, "is this one room illuminated — and all the others in darkness?"

Even then the significance of this circumstance was not apparent to me. But Holmes stared critically at an electric switch which was placed on the immediate right of the door and then up at the silk-shaded lantern which lighted the room. Crossing, he raised and lowered the switch rapidly, but the lamp continued to burn uninterruptedly!

"Ah!" he said — "a good trick!"

Grasping the wooden block to which the switch was attached, he turned it bodily — and I saw that it was a masked knob; for in the next moment he had pulled open the narrow section of wall — which proved to be nothing less than a cunningly fitted door!

A small, dimly lighted apartment was revealed, the Oriental note still predominant in its appointments, which, however, were few, and which I scarcely paused to note. For lying upon a mattress in this place was a pretty, fair-haired girl!

She lay on her side, having one white arm thrown out and resting limply on the floor, and she seemed to be in a semi-conscious condition, for although her fine eyes were widely opened, they had a glassy, witless look, and she was evidently unaware of our presence.

"Look at her pupils," rapped Holmes. "They have drugged her with bhang! Poor, pretty fool!"

"Good God!" I cried. "Who is this, Holmes?"

"Molly Clayton!" he answered. "Thank heaven we have saved one victim from Professor Moriarty."

V.

THE HAREM AGENCY

Owing to the instrumentality of Sherlock Holmes, the public never learned that the awful riverside murder called by the Press in reference to the victim's shaven skull "The Barber Atrocity" had any relation to the Deepbrow Kidnapping case. It was physically impossible to identify the victim, and Holmes had his own reasons for concealing the truth. The house on the wharf with its choice Oriental furniture was seized by the police; but, strange to relate, no arrest was made in connection with this most gruesome outrage. The man who dropped through the trap had been wounded by one of Holmes's shots, and he sank for the last time under the very eyes of the crew of the police cutter.

It was at a late hour on the night of this concluding tragedy that I learned the amazing truth underlying the case. Lestrade was still at work in the East End upon the hundred and one formalities which attached to his office, while Holmes and I sat in the study of our chambers in Baker Street.

"You see," Holmes was explaining. "After out debacle at Reichenbach Falls, the world thought I was dead. Was it not likely that Professor Moriarty, if he survived, should also keep that knowledge private. That he would confine his operations to parts of the world where I a not likely to sojourn?

"As to the kidnapping case, I got my first clue down at Deepbrow. The tracks leading to the Phaeton. They showed — to anyone not hampered by a preconceived opinion —

that the girl and Vane had not gone on together (since the man's footprints proved him to have been running), but that she had gone first and that he had run after her!

"Arguments: (a) He heard the approach of the carriage; or (b) he heard her call for help. In fact, it almost immediately became evident to me that someone else had met her at the end of the lane; probably someone who expected her, and whom she was going to meet when she, accidentally, encountered Vane! The captain was not attired for an elopement, and, more significant still, he said he should stroll to the Deep Wood, and that was where he did stroll to; for it borders the road at this point!

"I had privately ascertained, from the postman, that Molly Clayton actually received a letter on that morning! This resolved my last doubt. She was not going to meet Vane on the night of her disappearance.

"Then whom?"

"The old love! He who some months earlier had had over fifty seductive pictures of this undoubtedly pretty girl prepared for a purpose of his own! The handsome scoundrel that Moriarty used for 'recruiting' ..."

"And Vane interfered?"

"When the girl saw that they meant to take her away, she no doubt made a fuss! He ran to the rescue! They had not reckoned on his being there, but these are clever villains, who leave no clues — except for one who has met them on their own ground!"

"On their own ground! What do you mean, Holmes? What is the meaning of all this business? What do you mean by 'recruiting'?"

"Well — where do you suppose those fifty photographs went?"

"I cannot conjecture!"

"Then I will tell you. The turmoil in the East has put wealth and power into unscrupulous hands. But even before the war there were marts, Watson — open marts — at which a black girl might be purchased for some 30 pounds, and a Caucasian for anything from 250 pounds to 500 pounds! Ah! You stare! But I assure you it was so.

"Here is the point, though: there were, and still are, private dealers in women! Those photographs were circulated among the *nouveaux riches* of the East! They were employed in the same way that any other merchant employs a catalogue. They reached the hands of many an opulent and abandoned 'profiteer' of Damascus, Istanbul — where you will.

"Molly's picture would be one of many. Remember that hundreds of pretty girls disappear from their homes — taking the whole of the world — every year. Clearly, English beauty is popular at the moment!

"And," he added bitterly, "the arch-villain has escaped!"

"Professor Moriarty!" I cried. "Then Professor Moriarty ... "

"... Among his many other criminal activities, he is the biggest slave-dealer in the East!"

"Good God! Holmes — at last I understand!"

Holmes sighed.

"I was slow enough to understand it myself, Watson. But once the theory presented itself, I asked Lestrade to get into immediate touch with the valet he had already interviewed at Deepbrow. It was the result of his inquiry to which he referred when we met him at Scotland Yard tonight. Captain Vane had a large mole on his shoulder and a girl's name, together with a small device, tattooed on his forearm — a freak of his Sandhurst days."

"Then 'the man with the shaven skull' — "

"Is Captain Ronald Vane! May he rest in peace. But I never shall until that master of all that's evil in humanity has met Justice."

The Affair of the Chinaman's Pigtail

A most unusual adventure of Dr. Watson's
in which Sherlock Holmes does not appear

I.

HOW I OBTAINED IT

After the death of my beloved wife Mary, I was prone to having more time on my hands than I cared for, and being alone in the living quarters which I had shared with her led to thoughts and memories that were too painful for recollection. Accordingly, I took to "slumming" in various low parts of London where my professional life seldom carried me. On the evening in question, I was determined to visit Limehouse, that mysterious and oriental district so different from that encountered daily by the typical Englishman.

Leaving the dock gates behind me I tramped through the steady drizzle, going parallel with the river and making for the Chinese quarter. The hour was about half-past eleven on one of those September nights when, in such a locality as this, a stifling quality seems to enter the atmosphere, rendering it all but unbreathable. A mist floated over the river, and it was difficult to say if the rain was still falling, indeed, or if the ample moisture upon my garments was traceable only to the fog. Sounds were muffled, lights dimmed, and the frequent hooting of sirens from the river added another touch of weirdness to the scene.

Even when the peculiar duties of my friend, Sherlock Holmes, called him away from England, the lure of this miniature Orient which I had first explored under his guidance, often called me from my chambers. In the "House with Two Doors" in Wade Street, Limehouse, I would discard the armour of respectability, and, dressed in a manner unlikely to provoke comment in dockland, would haunt those dreary ways sometimes from midnight until close upon dawn. Yet, well as I knew the district and the strange and often dangerous creatures lurking in its many burrows, I experienced a chill partly physical and partly of apprehension to-night; indeed, strange though it may sound, I hastened my footsteps in order the sooner to reach the low den for which I was bound — Malay Jack's — a spot marked plainly on the crimes-map and which few respectable travellers would have regarded as a haven of refuge.

But the chill of the adjacent river, and some quality of utter desolation which seemed to emanate from the deserted wharves and ramshackle buildings about me, were driving me thither now; for I knew that human companionship, of a sort, and a glass of good liquor — from a store which the Customs would have been happy to locate — awaited me there. I might chance, too, upon Durham or Wessex, of New Scotland Yard, both good friends of mine, or even upon the Terror of Chinatown, Chief Inspector Kerry, a man for whom I had an esteem which none of his ungracious manners could diminish.

I was just about to turn to the right into a narrow and nameless alley, lying at right angles to the Thames, when I pulled up sharply, clenching my fists and listening.

A confused and continuous sound, not unlike that which might be occasioned by several large and savage hounds at close grips, was proceeding out of the darkness ahead of me; a worrying, growling, and scuffling which presently I identified as human, although in fact it was animal enough. A moment I hesitated, then, distinguishing among the sounds of conflict an unmistakable, though subdued, cry for help, I leaped forward and found myself in the midst of the melee. This was taking place in the lee of a high, dilapidated brick wall. A lamp in a sort of iron bracket spluttered dimly above on the right, but the scene of the conflict lay in densest shadow, so that the figures were indistinguishable.

"Help! By Gawd! they're strangling me — "

From almost at my feet the cry arose and was drowned in Chinese chattering. But guided by it I now managed to make out that the struggle in progress waged between a burly English sailorman and two lithe Chinese. The Oriental men seemed to have gained the advantage and my course was clear.

A straight right on the jaw of the Chinaman who was engaged in endeavouring to throttle the victim laid him prone in the dirty roadway. His companion, who was holding the wrist of the recumbent man, sprang upright as though propelled by a spring. I struck out at him savagely. He uttered a shrill scream not unlike that of a stricken hare, and fled so rapidly that he seemed to melt in the mist.

"Gawd bless you, mate!" came chokingly from the ground — and the rescued man, extricating himself from beneath the body of his stunned assailant, rose unsteadily to his feet and lurched toward me.

86

As I had surmised, he was a sailor, wearing a rough, blue-serge jacket and having his greasy trousers thrust into heavy seaboots — by which I judged that he was but newly come ashore. He stooped and picked up his cap. It was covered in mud, as were the rest of his garments, but he brushed it with his sleeve as though it had been but slightly soiled and clapped it on his head.

He grasped my hand in a grip of iron, peering into my face, and his breath was eloquent.

"I'd had one or two drinks, mate," he confided huskily (the confession was unnecessary). "It was them two in the Blue Anchor as did it; if I 'adn't 'ad them last two, I could 'ave broke up them blasted Chinamans with one 'and tied behind me."

"That's all right," I said hastily, "but what are we going to do about this Chinaman here?" I added, endeavouring at the same time to extricate my hand from the vise-like grip in which he persistently held it. "He hit the tiles pretty heavy when he went down."

As if to settle my doubts, the recumbent figure suddenly arose and without a word fled into the darkness and was gone like a phantom. My new friend made no attempt to follow, but:

"You can't kill a bloody Chinaman," he confided, still clutching my hand; "it ain't 'umanly possible. It's easier to kill a cat. Come along o' me and 'ave one; then I'll tell you somethink. I'll put you on somethink, I will."

With surprising steadiness of gait, considering the liquid cargo he had aboard, the man, releasing my hand and now seizing me firmly by the arm, confidently led me by divers narrow ways, which I knew, to a little beerhouse frequented by persons of his class.

My own attire was such as to excite no suspicion in these surroundings, and although I considered that my acquaintance had imbibed more than enough for one night, I let him have his own way in order that I might learn the story which he seemed disposed to confide in me. Settled in the corner of the beerhouse — which chanced to be nearly empty — with portentous pewters before us, the conversation was opened by my new friend:

"I've been paid off from the Jupiter — Samuelson's Planet Line," he explained. "What I am is a fireman."

"She was from Singapore to London?" I asked.

"She was," he replied, "and it was at Suez it 'appened — at Suez."

I did not interrupt him.

"I was ashore at Suez — we all was, owin' to a 'itch with the canal company — a matter of money, I may say. They make yer pay before they'll take yer through. Do you know that?"

I nodded.

"Suez is a place," he continued, "where they don't sell whisky, only poison. Was you ever at Suez?"

Again I nodded, being most anxious to avoid diverting the current of my friend's thoughts.

"Well, then," he continued, "you know Greek Jimmy's — and that's where I'd been."

I did not know Greek Jimmy's, but I thought it unnecessary to mention the fact.

"It was just about this time on a steamin' 'ot night as I come out of Jimmy's and started for the ship. I was walkin' along the Waghorn Quay, same as I might be walkin' along to-night, all by myself — bit of a list to port but nothing much — full o' joy an' happiness, 'appy an' free — 'appy an' free. Just like you might have noticed to-night, I noticed a knot of Chinamans scrappin' on the ground all amongst the dust right in front of me. I rammed in, windmillin' all round and knocking 'em down like skittles. Seemed to me there was about ten of 'em, but allowin' for Jimmy's whisky, maybe there wasn't more than three. Anyway, they all shifted and left me standin' there in the empty street with this 'ere in my 'and."

At that, without more ado, he thrust his hand deep into some concealed pocket and jerked out a Chinese pigtail, which had been severed, apparently some three inches from the scalp, by a clean cut. My acquaintance, with somewhat bleared eyes glistening in appreciation of his own dramatic skill — for I could not conceal my surprise — dangled it before me triumphantly.

"Which of 'em it belong to," he continued, thrusting it into another pocket and drumming loudly on the counter for more beer, "I can't say, 'cos I don't know. But that ain't all."

The tankards being refilled and my friend having sampled the contents of his own:

"That ain't all," he continued. "I thought I'd keep it as a sort of relic, like. What 'appened? I'll tell you. Amongst the crew there's three Chinamans — see? We ain't through the canal before one of 'em, a new one to me — Li Ping is his name — offers me five bob for the pigtail, which he sees me looking at one mornin'. I give him a punch on the nose an' 'e don't renew the offer: but that night (we're layin' at Port Said) 'e tries to pinch it! I dam' near broke his neck, and 'e don't try any more. To-night" — he extended his right arm forensically — "a deppitation of Chinamans waits on me at the dock gates; they explains as from a patriotic point of view they feels it to be their dooty to buy that pigtail off of me, and they bids a quid, a bar of gold — a Jimmy o' Goblin!"

He snapped his fingers contemptuously and emptied his pewter. A sense of what was coming began to dawn on me. That the "hold-up" near the riverside formed part of the scheme was possible, and, reflecting on my rough treatment of the two Chinamen, I chuckled inwardly. Possibly, however, the scheme had germinated in my acquaintance's mind merely as a result of an otherwise common assault, of a kind not unusual in these parts, but, whether elaborate or comparatively simple, that the story of the pigtail was a "plant" designed to reach my pocket, seemed a reasonable hypothesis.

"I told him to go to China," concluded the object of my suspicion, again rapping upon the counter, "and you see what come of it. All I got to say is this: If they're so bloody patriotic, I says one thing: I ain't the man to stand in their way. You done me a good turn to-night, mate; I'm doing you one. 'Ere's the bloody pigtail, 'ere's my empty mug. Fill the mug and the pigtail's yours. It's good for a quid at the dock gates any day!'"

My suspicions vanished; my interest arose to boiling point. I refilled my acquaintance's mug, pressed a sovereign upon him (in honesty I must confess that he was loath to take it), and departed with the pigtail coiled neatly in an inner pocket of my jacket. I entered the house in Wade Street by the side door, and half an hour later let myself out by the front door, having cast off my dockland disguise.

II.

HOW I LOST IT

It was not until the following evening that I found leisure to examine my strange acquisition, for affairs of more immediate importance engrossed my attention. But at about ten o'clock I seated myself at my table, lighted the lamp, and taking out the pigtail from the table drawer, placed it on the blotting-pad and began to examine it with the greatest curiosity, for few Chinese affect the pigtail nowadays.

I had scarcely commenced my examination, however, when it was dramatically interrupted. The door bell commenced to ring jerkily. I stood up, and as I did so the ringing ceased and in its place came a muffled beating on the door. I hurried into the passage as the bell commenced ringing again, and I had almost reached the door when once more the ringing ceased; but now I could hear a woman's voice, low but agitated:

"Open the door! Oh, for God's sake be quick!"

Completely mystified, and not a little alarmed, I threw open the door, and in there staggered a woman heavily veiled, so that I could see little of her features, but by the lines of her figure I judged her to be young.

Uttering a sort of moan of terror she herself closed the door, and stood with her back to it, watching me through the thick veil, while her breast rose and fell tumultuously.

"Thank God there was someone at home!" she gasped.

I think I may say with justice that I had never been so surprised in my life; every particular of the incident marked it as unique — set it apart from the episodes of everyday life.

"Madam," I began doubtfully, "you seem to be much alarmed at something, and if I can be of any assistance to you — "

"You have saved my life!" she whispered, and pressed one hand to her bosom. "In a moment I will explain."

"Won't you rest a little after your evidently alarming experience?" I suggested.

My strange visitor nodded, without speaking, and I conducted her to the study which I had just left, and placed the most comfortable armchair close beside the table so that as I sat I might study this woman who so strangely had burst in upon me. I even tilted the shaded lamp, artlessly, a trick I had learned from Holmes, in order that the light might fall upon her face.

She may have detected this device; I know not; but as if in answer to its challenge, she raised her gloved hands and unfastened the heavy veil which had concealed her features.

Thereupon I found myself looking into a pair of lustrous black eyes whose almond shape was that of the Orient; I found myself looking at a woman who, since she was evidently a Jewess, was probably no older than eighteen or nineteen, but whose beauty was ripely voluptuous, who might fittingly have posed for Salome, who, despite her modern fashionable garments, at once suggested to my mind the wanton beauty of the daughter of Herodias.

I stared at her silently for a time, and presently her full lips parted in a slow smile. My ideas were diverted into another channel.

"You have yet to tell me what alarmed you," I said in a low voice, but as courteously as possible, "and if I can be of any assistance in the matter."

My visitor seemed to recollect her fright — or the necessity for simulation. The pupils of her fine eyes seemed to grow larger and darker; she pressed her white teeth into her lower lips, and resting her hands upon the table leaned toward me.

"I am a stranger to London," she began, now exhibiting a certain diffidence, "and to-night I was looking for the chambers of Mr. Raphael Philips of Figtree Court."

"This is Figtree Court," I said, "but I certainly know of no Mr. Raphael Philips who has chambers here."

The black eyes met mine despairingly.

"But I am positive of the address!" protested my beautiful but strange caller — from her left glove she drew out a scrap of paper, "here it is."

I glanced at the fragment, upon which, in a woman's hand the words were pencilled: "Mr. Raphael Philips, 36-b Figtree Court, London."

I stared at my visitor, deeply mystified.

"These chambers are 36-b!" I said. "But I am not Raphael Philips, nor have I ever heard of him. My name is Dr. John Watson. There is evidently some mistake, but" — returning the slip of paper — "pardon me if I remind you, I have yet to learn the cause of your alarm."

"I was followed across the court and up the stairs."

"Followed! By whom?"

"By a dreadful-looking man, chattering in some tongue I did not understand!"

My amazement was momentarily growing greater.

"What kind of a man?" I demanded rather abruptly.

"A pallid-faced man — remember I could only just distinguish him in the darkness on the stairway, and see little more of him than his eyes at that, and his ugly gleaming teeth — oh! it was horrible!"

"You astound me," I said; "the thing is utterly incomprehensible." I switched off the light of the lamp. "I'll see if there's any sign of him in the court below."

"Oh, don't leave me! For heaven's sake don't leave me alone!"

She clutched my arm in the darkness.

"Have no fear; I merely propose to look out from this window."

Suiting the action to the word, I peered down into the court below. It was quite deserted. The night was a very dark one, and there were many patches of shadow in which a man might have lain concealed.

"I can see no one," I said, speaking as confidently as possible, and relighting the lamp, "if I call a cab for you and see you safely into it, you will have nothing to fear, I think."

"I have a cab waiting," she replied, and lowering the veil, she stood up to go.

"Kindly allow me to see you to it. I am sorry you have been subjected to this annoyance, especially as you have not attained the object of your visit."

"Thank you so much for your kindness; there must be some mistake about the address, of course."

She clung to my arm very tightly as we descended the stairs, and often glanced back over her shoulder affrightedly, as we crossed the court. There was not a sign of anyone about, however, and I could not make up my mind whether the story of the pallid man was a delusion or a fabrication. I inclined to the latter theory, but the object of such a deception was more difficult to determine.

Sure enough, a taxicab was waiting at the entrance to the court; and my visitor, having seated herself within, extended her hand to me, and even through the thick veil I could detect her brilliant smile.

"Thank you so much, Dr. Watson," she said, "and a thousand apologies. I am sincerely sorry to have given you all this trouble."

The cab drove off. For a moment I stood looking after it, in a state of dreamy incertitude, then turned and slowly retraced my steps. Reopening the door of my chambers with my key, I returned to my study and sat down at the table to endeavour to arrange the facts of what I recognized to be a really amazing episode. The adventure, trifling though it seemed, undoubtedly held some hidden significance that at present was not apparent to me. In accordance with the excellent custom of my friend, Sherlock Holmes, I prepared to make notes of the occurrence while the facts were still fresh in my memory. At the moment that I was about to begin, I made an astounding discovery.

Although I had been absent only a few minutes, and had locked my door behind me, the pigtail was gone!

I sat quite still, listening intently. The woman's story of the pale man on the stairs suddenly assumed a totally different aspect — a new and sinister aspect. Could it be that the pigtail was at the bottom of the mystery? — could it be that some murderous Chinaman who had been lurking in hiding, waiting his opportunity, had in some way gained access to my chambers during that brief absence? If so, was he gone?

From the table drawer I took out a revolver, ascertained that it was fully loaded, and turning up light after light as I proceeded, conducted a room-to-room search. It was without result; there was absolutely nothing to indicate that anyone had surreptitiously entered or departed from my chambers.

I returned to the study and sat gazing at the revolver lying on the blotting-pad before me. Perhaps my mind worked slowly, but I think that fully fifteen minutes must have passed before it dawned on me that the explanation not only of the missing pigtail but of the other incidents of the night, was simple enough. The pallid man had been a fabrication, and my dark-eyed visitor had not been in quest of "Raphael Philips," but in quest of the pigtail: and her quest had been successful!

"What a hopeless fool I am!" I cried, and banged my fist down upon the table, "there was no pale man at all — there was — "

My door bell rang. I sprang nervously to my feet, glanced at the revolver on the table — and finally dropped it into my coat pocket ere going out and opening the door.

On the landing stood a police constable and an officer in plain clothes.

"Your name is Dr. John Watson?" asked the constable, glancing at a note-book which he held in his hand.

"It is," I replied.

"You are required to come at once to Bow Street to identify a woman who was found murdered in a taxi-cab in the Strand about eleven o'clock to-night."

I suppressed an exclamation of horror, and I felt myself turning pale.

"But what has it to do — "

"The driver stated she came from your chambers, for you saw her off, and her last words to you were 'Good night, Dr. Watson, I am sincerely sorry to have given you all this trouble.' Is that correct, sir?"

The constable, who had read out the information in an official voice, now looked at me, as I stood there stupefied.

"It is," I said blankly. "I'll come at once." It would seem that I had misjudged my unfortunate visitor: her story of the pallid man on the stair had apparently been not a fabrication, but a gruesome fact!

III.

HOW I REGAINED IT

My ghastly duty was performed; I had identified the dreadful thing, which less than an hour before had been a strikingly beautiful woman, as my mysterious visitor. The police were palpably disappointed at the sparsity of my knowledge respecting her. In fact, had it not chanced that Detective Sergeant Durham was in the station, I think they would have doubted the accuracy of my story.

As a man of some experience in such matters, I fully recognized its improbability, but beyond relating the circumstances leading up to my possession of the pigtail and the events which had ensued, I could do no more in the matter. The weird relic had not been found on the dead woman, nor in the cab.

Now the unsavoury business was finished, and I walked along Bow Street, racking my mind for the master-key to this mystery in which I was become enmeshed. How I longed to rush off to Holmes's rooms in Baker Street and to tell him the whole story! But my friend was a thousand miles away — and I had to see the thing out alone.

That the pigtail was some sacred relic stolen from a Chinese temple and sought for by its fanatical custodians was a theory which persistently intruded itself. But I could find no place in that hypothesis for the beautiful Jewess; and that she was intimately concerned I did not doubt. A cool survey of the facts rendered it fairly evident that it was she and none other who had stolen the pigtail from my rooms. Some third party — possibly the "pallid man" of whom she had spoken

— had in turn stolen it from her, strangling her in the process.

The police theory of the murder (and I was prepared to accept it) was that the assassin had been crouching in hiding behind or beside the cab — or even within the dark interior. He had leaped in and attacked the woman at the moment that the taxi-man had started his engine; if already inside, the deed had proven even easier. Then, during some block in the traffic, he had slipped out unseen, leaving the body of the victim to be discovered when the cab pulled up at the hotel.

I knew of only one place in London where I might hope to obtain useful information, and for that place I was making now. It was Malay Jack's, whence I had been bound on the previous night when my strange meeting with the seaman who then possessed the pigtail had led to a change of plan. The scum of the Asiatic population always come at one time or another to Jack's, and I hoped by dint of a little patience to achieve what the police had now apparently despaired of achieving — the discovery of the assassin.

Having called at my chambers to obtain my revolver, I mounted an eastward-bound motor-bus. The night, as I have already stated, was exceptionally dark. There was no moon, and heavy clouds were spread over the sky; so that the deserted East End streets presented a sufficiently uninviting aspect, but one with which I was by no means unfamiliar and which certainly in no way daunted me.

Changing at Sherlock Holmes's Chinatown base in Wade Street, I turned my steps in the same direction as upon the preceding night; but if my own will played no part in the matter, then decidedly Providence truly guided me.

Poetic justice is rare enough in real life, yet I was destined to-night to witness swift retribution overtaking a malefactor.

The by-ways which I had trodden were utterly deserted; I was far from the lighted high road, and the only signs of human activity that reached me came from the adjacent river; therefore, when presently an outcry arose from somewhere on my left, for a moment I really believed that my imagination was vividly reproducing the episode of the night before!

A furious scuffle — between a European and an Asiatic — was in progress not twenty yards away!

Realizing that such was indeed the case, and that I was not the victim of hallucination, I advanced slowly in the direction of the sounds, but my footsteps reechoed hollowly from wall to wall of the narrow passage-way, and my coming brought the conflict to a sudden and dramatic termination.

"Thought I wouldn't know yer ugly face, did yer?" yelled a familiar voice. "No good squealin' — I got yer! I'd bust you up if I could!" (a sound of furious blows and inarticulate chattering) "but it ain't 'umanly possible to kill a Chinaman — "

I hurried forward toward the spot where two dim figures were locked in deadly conflict.

"Take that to remember me by!" gasped the husky voice as I ran up.

One of the figures collapsed in a heap upon the ground. The other made off at a lumbering gait along a second and even narrower passage branching at right angles from that in which the scuffle had taken place.

The clatter of the heavy sea-boots died away in the distance. I stood beside the fallen man, looking keenly about to right and left; for an impression was strong upon me that another than I had been witness of the scene — that a shadowy form had slunk back furtively at my approach. But the night gave up no sound in confirmation of this, and I could detect no sign of any lurker.

I stooped over the Chinaman (for a Chinaman it was) who lay at my feet, and directed the ray of my pocket-lamp upon his pale and contorted countenance. I suppressed a cry of surprise and horror.

Despite the human impossibility referred to by the missing fireman, this particular Chinaman had joined the shades of his ancestors. I think that final blow, which had felled him, had brought his shaven skull in such violent contact with the wall that he had died of the thundering concussion set up.

Kneeling there and looking into his upturned eyes, I became aware that my position was not an enviable one, particularly since I felt little disposed to set the law on the track of the real culprit. For this man who now lay dead at my feet was doubtless one of the pair who had attempted the life of the fireman of the Jupiter.

That my seafaring acquaintance had designed to kill the Chinaman I did not believe, despite his stormy words: the death had been an accident, and (perhaps my morality was over-broad) I considered the assault to have been justified.

Now my ideas led me further yet. The dead Chinaman wore a rough blue coat, and gingerly, for I found the contact repulsive, I inserted my hand into the inside pocket. Immediately my fingers closed upon a familiar object — and I stood up, whistling slightly, and dangling in my left hand the missing pigtail!

Beyond doubt Justice had guided the seaman's blows. This was the man who had murdered my dark-eyed visitor!

I stood perfectly still, directing the little white ray of my flashlight upon the pigtail in my hand. I realized that my position, difficult before, now was become impossible; the possession of the pigtail compromised me hopelessly. What should I do?

"My God!" I said aloud, "what does it all mean?"

"It means," said a gruff voice, "that it was lucky I was following you and saw what happened!"

I whirled about, my heart leaping wildly. Detective-Sergeant Durham was standing watching me, a grim smile upon his face!

I laughed rather shakily.

"Lucky indeed!" I said. "Thank God you're here. This pigtail is a nightmare which threatens to drive me mad!"

The detective advanced and knelt beside the crumpled-up figure on the ground. He examined it briefly, and then stood up.

"The fact that he had the missing pigtail in his pocket," he said, "is proof enough to my mind that he did the murder."

"And to mine."

"There's another point," he added, "which throws a lot of light on the matter. You and Mr. Holmes were out of town at the time of the Huang Chow case; but the Chief and I outlined it, you remember, one night in Mr. Holmes's rooms?"

"I remember it perfectly; the giant spider in the coffin — "

"Yes; and a certain Ah Fu, confidential servant of the old man, who used to buy the birds the thing fed on. Well sir, Dr. Watson, Huang Chow was the biggest dealer in illicit stuff in all the East End — and this battered thing at our feet is — Ah Fu!"

"Huang Chow's servant?"

"Exactly!"

I stared, uncomprehendingly.

"In what way does this throw light on the matter?" I asked.

Durham — a very intelligent young officer — smiled significantly.

"I begin to see light!" he declared. "The gentleman who made off just as I arrived on the scene probably had a private quarrel with the Chinaman and was otherwise not concerned in any way."

"I am disposed to agree with you," I said guardedly.

"Of course, you've no idea of his identity?"

"I'm afraid not."

"We may find him," mused the officer, glancing at me shrewdly, "by applying at the offices of the Planet Line, but I rather doubt it. Also I rather doubt if we'll look very far. He's saved us a lot of trouble, but" — peering about in the shadowy corners which abounded — "didn't I see somebody else lurking around here?"

"I'm almost certain there was someone else!" I cried. "In fact, I could all but swear to it."

"H'm!" said the detective. "He's not here now. Might I trouble you to walk along to Limehouse Police Station for the ambulance? I'd better stay here."

I agreed at once, and started off.

Thus a second time my plans were interrupted, for my expedition that night ultimately led me to Bow Street, whence, after certain formalities had been observed, I departed for my chambers, the mysterious pigtail in my pocket. Failing the presence of Durham, the pigtail must have been retained as evidence, but:

"We shall know where to find it if it's wanted, Dr. Watson," said the Yard man, "and I can trust you to look after your own property."

The clock of St. Paul's was chiming the hour of two when I locked the door of my chambers and prepared to turn in.

106

The clangour of the final strokes yet vibrated through the night's silence when someone set my own door bell loudly ringing.

With an exclamation of annoyance I shot back the bolts and threw open the door.

A Chinaman stood outside upon the mat!

IV.

HOW IT ALL ENDED

"Me wishee see you," said the apparition, smiling blandly; "me comee in?"

"Come in, by all means," I said without enthusiasm, and, switching on the light in my study, I admitted the Chinaman and stood facing him with an expression upon my face which I doubt not was the reverse of agreeable.

My visitor, who wore a slop-shop suit, also wore a wide-brimmed bowler hat; now, the set bland smile still upon his pallid face, he removed the bowler and pointed significantly to his skull.

His pigtail had been severed some three inches from the root!

"You gotchee my pigtail," he explained; "me callee get it — thank you."

"Thank you," I said grimly. "But I must ask you to establish your claim rather more firmly."

"Yessir," agreed the Chinaman.

And thereupon in tolerable pidgin English he unfolded his tale. He proclaimed his name to be Hi Wing Ho, and his profession that of a sailor, or so I understood him. While ashore at Suez he had become embroiled with some drunken seamen: knives had been drawn, and in the scuffle by some strange accident his pigtail had been severed. He had escaped from the conflict, badly frightened, and had run a great distance before he realized his loss. Since Southern Chinamen of his particular Tong hold their pigtails in the highest regard, he had instituted inquiries as soon as possible, and had presently learned from a Chinese member of the crew of the S.S. Jupiter that the precious queue had fallen into the hands of a fireman on that vessel. He (Hi Wing Ho) had shipped on the first available steamer bound for England, having in the meanwhile communicated with his friend on the Jupiter respecting the recovery of the pigtail.

"What was the name of your friend on the Jupiter?"

"Him Li Ping — yessir!" — without the least hesitation or hurry.

I nodded. "Go on," I said.

He arrived at the London docks very shortly after the Jupiter. Indeed, the crew of the latter vessel had not yet been paid off when Hi Wing Ho presented himself at the dock gates. He admitted that, finding the fireman so obdurate, he and his friend Li Ping had resorted to violence, but he did not seem to recognize me as the person who had frustrated their designs. Thus far I found his story credible enough, excepting the accidental severing of the pigtail at Suez, but now it became wildly improbable, for he would have me believe that Li Ping, or Ah Fu, obtaining possession of the pigtail (in what manner Hi Wing Ho protested that he knew not) he sought to hold it to ransom, knowing how highly Hi Wing Ho valued it.

I glared sternly at the Chinaman, but his impassive countenance served him well. That he was lying to me I no longer doubted; for Ah Fu could not have hoped to secure such a price as would justify his committing murder; furthermore, the presence of the unfortunate Jewess in the case was not accounted for by the ingenious narrative of Hi Wing Ho. I was standing staring at him and wondering what course to adopt, when yet again my restless door-bell clamoured in the silence.

Hi Wing Ho started nervously, exhibiting the first symptoms of alarm which I had perceived in him. My mind was made up in an instant. I took my revolver from the drawer and covered him.

"Be good enough to open the door, Hi Wing Ho," I said coldly.

He shrank from me, pouring forth voluble protestations.

"Open the door!"

I clenched my left fist and advanced upon him. He scuttled away with his odd Chinese gait and threw open the door. Standing before me I saw my friend Detective Sergeant Durham, and with him a remarkably tall and very large-boned man whose square-jawed face was deeply tanned and whose aspect was dourly Scottish.

When the piercing eyes of this stranger rested upon Hi Wing Ho an expression which I shall never forget entered into them; an expression coldly murderous. As for the Chinaman, he literally crumpled up.

"You rat!" roared the stranger.

Taking one long stride he stooped upon the Chinaman, seized him by the back of the neck as a terrier might seize a rat, and lifted him to his feet.

"The mystery of the pigtail, Dr. Watson," said the detective, "is solved at last."

"Have ye got it?" demanded the Scotsman, turning to me, but without releasing his hold upon the neck of Hi Wing Ho.

I took the pigtail from my pocket and dangled it before his eyes.

"Suppose you come into my study," I said, "and explain matters."

We entered the room which had been the scene of so many singular happenings. The detective and I seated ourselves, but the Scotsman, holding the Chinaman by the neck as though he had been some inanimate bundle, stood just within the doorway, one of the most gigantic specimens of manhood I had ever set eyes upon.

"You do the talking, sir," he directed the detective; "ye have all the facts."

While Durham talked, then, we all listened — excepting the Chinaman, who was past taking an intelligent interest in anything, and who, to judge from his starting eyes, was being slowly strangled.

"The gentleman," said Durham — "Mr. Nicholson — arrived two days ago from the East. He is a buyer for a big firm of diamond merchants, and some weeks ago a valuable diamond was stolen from him — "

"By this!" interrupted the Scotsman, shaking the wretched Hi Wing Ho terrier fashion.

"By Hi Wing Ho," explained the detective, "whom you see before you. The theft was a very ingenious one, and the man succeeded in getting away with his haul. He tried to dispose of the diamond to a certain Isaac Cohenberg, a Singapore moneylender; but Isaac Cohenberg was the bigger crook of the two. Hi Wing Ho only escaped from the establishment of Cohenberg by dint of sandbagging the moneylender, and quitted the town by a boat which left the same night. On the voyage he was indiscreet enough to take the diamond from its hiding-place and surreptitiously to examine it. Another member of the Chinese crew, one Li Ping — otherwise Ah Fu, the accredited agent of old Huang Chow! — was secretly watching our friend, and, knowing that he possessed this valuable jewel, he also learned where he kept it hidden. At Suez Ah Fu attacked Hi Wing Ho and secured possession of the diamond. It was to secure possession of the diamond that Ah Fu had gone out East. I don't doubt it. He employed Hi Wing Ho — and Hi Wing Ho tried to double on him!

"We are indebted to you, Dr. Watson, for some of the data upon which we have reconstructed the foregoing and also for the next link in the narrative. A fireman ashore from the Jupiter intruded upon the scene at Suez and deprived Ah Fu of the fruits of his labours. Hi Wing Ho seems to have been badly damaged in the scuffle, but Ah Fu, the more wily of the two, evidently followed the fireman, and, deserting from his own ship, signed on with the Jupiter."

While this story was enlightening in some respects, it was mystifying in others. I did not interrupt, however, for Durham immediately resumed:

"The drama was complicated by the presence of a fourth character — the daughter of Cohenberg. Realizing that a small fortune had slipped through his fingers, the old moneylender dispatched his daughter in pursuit of Hi Wing Ho, having learned upon which vessel the latter had sailed. He had no difficulty in obtaining this information, for he is in touch with all the crooks of the town. Had he known that the diamond had been stolen by an agent of Huang Chow, he would no doubt have hesitated. Huang Chow has an international reputation.

"However, his daughter — a girl of great personal beauty — relied upon her diplomatic gifts to regain possession of the stone, but, poor creature, she had not counted with Ah Fu, who was evidently watching your chambers (while Hi Wing Ho, it seems, was assiduously shadowing Ah Fu!). How she traced the diamond from point to point of its travels we do not know, and probably never shall know, but she was undeniably clever and unscrupulous. Poor girl! She came to a dreadful end. Mr. Nicholson, here, identified her at Bow Street to-night."

Now the whole amazing truth burst upon me.

"I understand!" I cried. "This" — and I snatched up the pigtail —

"That my pigtail," moaned Hi Wing Ho feebly.

Mr. Nicholson pitched him unceremoniously into a corner of the room, and taking the pigtail in his huge hand, clumsily unfastened it. Out from the thick part, some two inches below the point at which it had been cut from the Chinaman's head, a great diamond dropped upon the floor!

For perhaps twenty seconds there was perfect silence in my study. No one stooped to pick the diamond from the floor — the diamond which now had blood upon it. No one, so far as my sense informed me, stirred. But when, following those moments of stupefaction, we all looked up — Hi Wing Ho, like a phantom, had faded from the room!

The Affair of the Golden Idol

I.

THE BLOOD-STAINED STATUE

"Stop when we pass the next lamp and give me a light for my pipe."

"Why?"

"No! don't look round," warned my companion. "I think someone is following us. And it is always advisable to be on guard in this neighbourhood."

We had nearly reached the house in Wade Street, Limehouse, which my friend used as a base for East End operations. The night was dark but clear, and I thought that presently when dawn came it would bring a cold, bright morning. There was no moon, and as we passed the lamp and paused we stood in almost total darkness.

Facing in the direction of the Council School I struck a match. It revealed my ruffianly looking companion — in whom his nearest friends must have failed to recognize Mr. Sherlock Holmes of Baker Street.

He was glancing furtively back along the street, and when a moment later we moved on, I too, had detected the presence of a figure stumbling toward us.

"Don't stop at the door," whispered Holmes, for our follower was only a few yards away.

Accordingly we passed the house in which Holmes had rooms, and had proceeded some fifteen paces farther when the man who was following us stumbled in between Holmes and myself, clutching an arm of either. I scarcely knew what to expect, but was prepared for anything, when he spoke.

"Mates!" said a man huskily. "Mates, if you know where I can get a drink, take me there!"

Holmes laughed shortly. I cannot say if he remained suspicious of the newcomer, but for my own part I had determined after one glance at the man that he was merely a drunken fireman newly recovered from a prolonged debauch.

"Where 'ave yer been, old son?" growled Holmes, in that wonderful Cockney dialect of his which I had so often and so vainly sought to cultivate. "You look as though you'd 'ad one too many already."

"I ain't," declared the fireman, who appeared to be in a semi-dazed condition. "I ain't 'ad one since ten o'clock last night. It's dope wot's got me, not rum."

"Dope!" said Holmes sharply; "been 'avin' a pipe, eh?"

"If you've got a corpse-reviver anywhere," continued the man in that curious, husky voice, "'ave pity on me, mate. I seen a thing to-night wot give me the jim-jams."

"All right, old son," said my friend good-humouredly; "about turn! I've got a drop in the bottle, but me an' my mate sails to-morrow, an' it's the last."

116

"Gawd bless yer!" growled the fireman; and the three of us — an odd trio, truly — turned about, retracing our steps.

As we approached the street lamp and its light shone upon the haggard face of the man walking between us, Holmes stopped.

"Wot's up with yer eye?" he inquired.

Holmes suddenly tilted the man's head upward and peered closely into one of his eyes. I suppressed a gasp of surprise for I instantly recognized the fireman of the Jupiter who once gave me a Chinaman's pigtail!

"Nothin' up with it, is there?" said the fireman.

"Only a lump o' mud," growled Holmes, and with a very dirty handkerchief he pretended to remove the imaginary stain, and then, turning to me:

"Open the door, Jim," he directed.

His examination of the man's eyes had evidently satisfied him that our acquaintance had really been smoking opium.

We paused immediately outside the "House with Two Doors" for which we had been bound, and as I had the key I opened the door and the three of us stepped into a little dark room. Holmes closed the door and we stumbled upstairs to a low first-floor apartment facing the street. There was nothing in its appointments, as revealed in the light of an oil lamp burning on the solitary table, to distinguish it from a thousand other such apartments which may be leased for a few shillings a week in the neighbourhood. That adjoining might have told a different story, for it more closely resembled an actor's dressing-room than a seaman's lodging; but the door of this sanctum was kept scrupulously locked.

"Sit down, old son," said my friend heartily, pushing forward an old armchair. "Fetch out the grog, Jim; there's about enough for three."

I walked to a cupboard, as the fireman sank limply down in the chair, and took out a bottle and three glasses. When the man, who, as I could now see quite plainly, was suffering from the after effects of opium, had eagerly gulped the stiff drink which I handed to him, he looked around with dim, glazed eyes.

"You've saved my life, mates," he declared. "I've 'ad a 'orrible nightmare, I 'ave — a nightmare. See?"

He fixed his eyes on me for a moment, then raised himself from his seat, peering narrowly at me across the table.

"I seed you before, mate. Gaw, blimey! if you ain't the bloke wot I giv'd the pigtail to! And wot laid out that blasted Chinaman as was scraggin' me! Shake, mate!"

I shook hands with him, Holmes eyeing me closely the while, in a manner which told me that his quick brain had already supplied the link connecting our doped acquaintance with my strange experience during his absence. At the same time it occurred to me that my fireman friend did not know that Ah Fu was dead, or he would never have broached the subject so openly.

"That's so," I said, and wondered if he required further information.

"It's all right, mate. I don't want to 'ear no more about blinking pigtails — not all my life I don't," and he sat back heavily in his chair and stared at Holmes.

"Where have you been?" inquired Holmes, as if no interruption had occurred, and then began to reload his pipe: "at Malay Jack's or at Number Fourteen?"

"Neither of 'em!" cried the fireman, some evidence of animation appearing in his face; "I been at Kwen Lung's."

"In Pennyfields?"

"That's 'im, the old bloke with the big Chinese idol. I allers goes to see Ma Lorenzo when I'm in Port o' London. I've seen 'er for the last time, mates."

He banged a big and dirty hand upon the table.

"Last night I see murder done, an' only that I know they wouldn't believe me, I'd walk across to Limehouse P'lice Station presently and put the splits on 'em, I would."

Holmes, who was seated behind the speaker, glanced at me significantly.

"Sure you wasn't dreamin'?" he inquired facetiously.

"Dreamin'!" cried the man. "Dreams don't leave no blood be'ind, do they?"

"Blood!" I exclaimed.

"That's wot I said — blood! When I woke up this mornin' there was blood all on that grinnin' Chinese idol — the blood wot 'ad dripped from 'er shoulders when she fell."

"Eh!" said Holmes. "Blood on whose shoulders? Wot the 'ell are you talkin' about, old son?"

"Ere" — the fireman turned in his chair and grasped Holmes by the arm — "listen to me, and I'll tell you somethink, I will. I'm goin' in the Seahawk in the mornin' see? But if you want to know somethink, I'll tell yer. Drunk or sober, I bars the blasted p'lice, but if you like to tell 'em I'll put you on somethink worth tellin'. Sure the bottle's empty, mates?"

I caught Holmes's glance and divided the remainder of the whisky evenly between the three glasses.

"Good 'ealth," said the fireman, and disposed of his share at a draught. "That's bucked me up wonderful."

He lay back in his chair and from a little tobacco-box began to fill a short clay pipe.

"Look 'ere, mates, I'm soberin' up, like, after the smoke, an' I can see, I can see plain, as nobody'll ever believe me. Nobody ever does, worse luck, but 'ere goes. Pass the matches."

He lighted his pipe, and looking about him in a sort of vaguely aggressive way:

"Last night," he resumed, "after I was chucked out of the Dock Gates, I made up my mind to go and smoke a pipe with old Ma Lorenzo. Round I goes to Pennyfields, and she don't seem glad to see me. There's nobody there only me. Not like the old days when you 'ad to book your seat in advance."

He laughed gruffly.

"She didn't want to let me in at first, said they was watched, that if a Chinaman 'ad an old pipe wot 'ad b'longed to 'is grandfather it was good enough to get 'im fined fifty quid. Anyway, me bein' an old friend she spread a mat for me and filled me a pipe. I asked after old Kwen Lung, but, of course, 'e was out gamblin', as usual; so after old Ma Lorenzo 'ad made me comfortable an' gone out I 'ad the place to myself, and presently I dozed off and forgot all about bloody ship's bunkers an' nigger-drivin' Scotchmen."

He paused and looked about him defiantly.

"I dunno 'ow long I slept," he continued, "but some time in the night I kind of 'alf woke up."

At that he twisted violently in his chair and glared across at Holmes:

"You been a pal to me," he said; "but tell me I was dreamin' again and I'll smash yer bloody face!"

He glared for a while, then addressing his narrative more particularly to me, he resumed:

"It was a scream wot woke me — a woman's scream. I didn't sit up; I couldn't. I never felt like it before. It was the same as bein' buried alive, I should think. I could see an' I could 'ear, but I couldn't move one muscle in my body. Foller me? An' wot did I see, mates, an' wot did I 'ear? I'm goin' to tell yer. I see old Kwen Lung's daughter — "

121

"I didn't know 'e 'ad one," murmured Holmes.

"Then you don't know much!" shouted the fireman. "I knew years ago, but 'e kept 'er stowed away somewhere up above, an' last night was the first time I ever see 'er. It was 'er shriek wot 'ad reached me, reached me through the smoke. I don't take much stock in Chinaman gals in general, but this one's mother was no Chinaman, I'll swear. She was just as pretty as a bloomin' ivory doll, an' as little an' as white, and that old swine Kwen Lung 'ad tore the dress off of 'er shoulders with a bloody great whip!"

Holmes was leaning forward in his seat now, intent upon the man's story, and although I could not get rid of the idea that our friend was relating the events of a particularly unpleasant opium dream, nevertheless I was fascinated by the strange story and by the strange manner of its telling.

"I saw the blood drip from 'er bare shoulders, mates," the man continued huskily, and with his big dirty hands he strove to illustrate his words. "An' that old Oriental devil lashed an' lashed until the poor gal was past screamin'. She just sunk down on the floor all of a 'cap, moanin' and moanin' — Gawd! I can 'ear 'er moanin' now!"

"Meanwhile, 'ere's me with murder in me 'eart lyin' there watchin', an' I can't speak, no! I can't even curse the pallid rat, an' I can't move — not a 'and, not a foot! Just as she fell there right up against the Chinese idol an' 'er blood trickled down on 'is gilded feet, old Ma Lorenzo comes staggerin' in. I remember all this as clear as print, mates, remember it plain, but wot 'appened next ain't so good an' clear. Somethink seemed to bust in me 'ead. Only just before I went off, the winder — there's only one in the room — was smashed to smithereens an' somebody come in through it."

"Are you sure?" said Holmes eagerly. "Are you sure?"

That he was intensely absorbed in the story he revealed by a piece of bad artistry, very rare in him. He temporarily forgot his dialect. Our marine friend, however, was too much taken up with his own story to notice the slip.

"Dead sure!" he shouted.

He suddenly twisted around in his chair.

"Tell me I was dreamin', mate," he invited, "and if you ain't dreamin' in 'arf a tick it won't be because I 'aven't put yer to sleep!"

"I ain't arguin', old son," said Holmes soothingly. "Get on with your yarn."

"Ho!" said the fireman, mollified, "so long as you ain't. Well, then, it's all blotted out after that. Somebody come in at the winder, but 'oo it was or wot it was I can't tell yer, not for fifty quid. When I woke up, which is about 'arf an hour before you see me, I'm all alone — see? There's no sign of Kwen Lung nor the gal nor old Ma Lorenzo nor anybody. I sez to meself, wot you keep on sayin'. I sez, 'You're dreamin', Bill.'"

"But I don't think you was," declared Holmes. "Straight I don't."

"I know I wasn't!" roared the fireman, and banged the table lustily. "I see 'er blood on the Chinese idol an' on the floor where she lay!"

"This morning?" I interjected.

"This mornin', in the light of the little oil lamp where old Ma Lorenzo 'ad roasted the pills! It's all still an' quiet an' I feel more dead than alive. I'm goin' to give 'er a hail, see? When I sez to myself, 'Bill,' I sez, 'put out to sea; you're amongst Kaffirs, Bill.' It occurred to me as old Kwen Lung might wonder 'ow much I knew. So I beat it. But when I got in the open air I felt I'd never make my lodgin's without a tonic. That's 'ow I come to meet you, mates.

"Listen — I'm away in the old Seahawk in the mornin', but I'll tell you somethink. That Oriental bastard killed his daughter last night! Beat 'er to death. I see it plain. The sweetest, prettiest bit of ivory as Gawd ever put breath into. If 'er body ain't in the river, it's in the 'ouse. Drunk or sober, I never could stand the splits, but mates" — he stood up, and grasping me by the arm, he drew me across the room where he also seized Holmes in his muscular grip — "mates," he went on earnestly, "she was the sweetest, prettiest little gal as a man ever clapped eyes on. One of yer walk into Limehouse Station an' put the koppers wise. I'd sleep easier at sea if I knew old Kwen Lung 'ad gone west on a bloody rope's end."

II.

AT KWEN LUNG'S

For fully ten minutes after the fireman had departed Sherlock Holmes sat staring abstractedly in front of him, his cold pipe between his teeth, and knowing his moods I intruded no words upon this reverie, until:

"Come on, Watson," he said, standing up suddenly, "I think this matter calls for speedy action."

"What! Do you think the man's story was true?"

"I think nothing. I am going to look at Kwen Lung's Chinese idol."

Without another word he led the way downstairs and out into the deserted street. The first gray halftones of dawn were creeping into the sky, so that the outlines of Limehouse loomed like dim silhouettes about us. There was abundant evidence in the form of noises, strange and discordant, that many workers were busy on dock and riverside, but the streets through which our course lay were almost empty. Sometimes a furtive shadow would move out of some black gully and fade into a dimly seen doorway in a manner peculiarly unpleasant and Asiatic. But we met no palpable pedestrian throughout the journey.

Before the door of a house in Pennyfields which closely resembled that which we had left in Wade Street, in that it was flatly uninteresting, dirty and commonplace, we paused. There was no sign of life about the place and no lights showed at any of the windows, which appeared as dim cavities — eyeless sockets in the gray face of the building, as dawn proclaimed the birth of a new day.

Holmes seized the knocker and knocked sharply. There was no response, and he repeated the summons, but again without effect. Thereupon, with a muttered exclamation, he grasped the knocker a third time and executed a veritable tattoo upon the door. When this had proceeded for about half a minute or more:

"All right, all right!" came a shaky voice from within. "I'm coming."

Holmes released the knocker, and, turning to me:

"Ma Lorenzo," he whispered. "Don't make any mistakes."

Indeed, even as he warned me, heralded by a creaking of bolts and the rattling of a chain, the door was opened by a fat, shapeless, half-caste woman of indefinite age; in whose dark eyes, now sunken in bloated cheeks, in whose full though drooping lips, and even in the whole overlaid contour of whose face and figure it was possible to recognize the traces of former beauty. This was Ma Lorenzo, who for many years had lived at that address with old Kwen Lung, of whom strange stories were told in Chinatown.

As Bill Jones, A.B., my friend, Sherlock Holmes, was well known to Ma Lorenzo as he was well known to many others in that strange colony which clusters round the London docks. I sometimes enjoyed the privilege of accompanying my friend on a tour of investigation through the weird resorts which abound in that neighbourhood, and, indeed, we had been returning from one of these Baghdad nights when our present adventure had been thrust upon us. Assuming a wild and boisterous manner which he had at command:

"'Urry up, Ma!" said Holmes, entering without ceremony; "I want to introduce my pal Jim 'ere to old Kwen Lung, and make it all right for him before I sail."

Ma Lorenzo, who was half Portuguese, replied in her peculiar accent:

"This no time to come waking me up out of bed!"

But Holmes, brushing past her, was already inside the stuffy little room, and I hastened to follow.

"Kwen Lung!" shouted my friend loudly. "Where are you? Brought a friend to see you."

"Kwen Lung no hab," came the complaining tones of Ma Lorenzo from behind us.

It was curious to note how long association with the Chinese had resulted in her catching the infection of that pidgin-English which is a sort of esperanto in all Asiatic quarters.

"Eh!" cried my friend, pushing open a door on the right of the passage and stumbling down three worn steps into a very evil-smelling room. "Where is he?"

"Go play fan-tan. Not come back."

Ma Lorenzo, having relocked the street door, had rejoined us, and as I followed my friend down into the dim and uninviting apartment she stood at the top of the steps, hands on hips, regarding us.

The place, which was quite palpably an opium den, must have disappointed anyone familiar with the more ornate houses of Chinese vice in San Francisco and elsewhere. The bare floor was not particularly clean, and the few decorations which the room boasted were garishly European for the most part. A deep divan, evidently used sometimes as a bed, occupied one side of the room, and just to the left of the steps reposed the only typically Oriental object in the place.

It was a strange thing to see in so sordid a setting; a great gilded Chinese idol, more than life-size, squatting, hideous, upon a massive pedestal; a figure fit for some native temple but strangely out of place in that dirty little Limehouse abode.

I had never before visited Kwen Lung's, but the fame of his golden Chinese idol had reached me, and I know that he had received many offers for it, all of which he had rejected. It was whispered that Kwen Lung was rich, that he was a great man among the Chinese, and even that some kind of religious ceremony periodically took place in his house. Now, as I stood staring at the famous idol, I saw something which made me stare harder than ever.

The place was lighted by a hanging lamp from which depended bits of coloured paper and several gilded silk tassels; but dim as the light was it could not conceal those tell-tale stains.

There was blood on the feet of the golden idol!

All this I detected at a glance, but ere I had time to speak:

"You can't tell me that tale, Ma!" cried Holmes. "I believe 'e was smokin' in 'ere when we knocked."

The woman shrugged her fat shoulders.

"No, hab," she repeated. "You two johnnies clear out. Let me sleep."

But as I turned to her, beneath the nonchalant manner I could detect a great uneasiness; and in her dark eyes there was fear. That Holmes also had seen the bloodstains I was well aware, and I did not doubt that furthermore he had noted the fact that the only mat which the room boasted had been placed before the Chinese idol — doubtless to hide other stains upon the boards.

As we stood so I presently became aware of a current of air passing across the room in the direction of the open door. It came from a window before which a tawdry red curtain had been draped. Either the window behind the curtain was wide open, which is alien to Chinese habits, or it was shattered. While I was wondering if Holmes intended to investigate further:

"Come on, Jim!" he cried boisterously, and clapped me on the shoulder; "the old fox don't want to be disturbed."

He turned to the woman:

"Tell him when he wakes up, Ma," he said, "that if ever my pal Jim wants a pipe he's to 'ave one. Savvy? Jim's square."

"Savvy," replied the woman, and she was wholly unable to conceal her relief. "You clear out now, and I tell Kwen Lung when he come in."

"Righto, Ma!" said Holmes. "Kiss 'im on both cheeks for me, an' tell 'im I'll be 'ome again in a month."

Grasping me by the arm he lurched up the steps, and the two of us presently found ourselves out in the street again. In the growing light the squalor of the district was more evident than ever, but the comparative freshness of the air was welcome after the reek of that room in which the golden idol sat leering, with blood at his feet.

"You saw, Holmes?" I exclaimed excitedly. "You saw the stains? And I'm certain the window was broken!"

Holmes nodded shortly.

"Back to Wade Street!" he said. "I allow myself fifteen minutes to shed Bill Jones, able seaman, and to become Sherlock Holmes, of Baker Street."

As we hurried along:

"What steps shall you take?" I asked.

"First step: search Kwen Lung's house from cellar to roof. Second step: entirely dependent upon result of first. The Chinese are subtle, Watson. If Kwen Lung has killed his daughter, it may require all the resources of Scotland Yard to prove it."

"But — "

"There is no 'but' about it. Chinatown is the one district of London which possesses the property of swallowing people up."

III.

"CAPTAIN DAN"

Half an hour later, as I sat in the inner room before the great dressing-table laboriously removing my disguise — for I was utterly incapable of metamorphosing myself like Holmes in seven minutes — I heard a rapping at the outer door. I glanced nervously at my face in the mirror.

Comparatively little of "Jim" had yet been removed, for since time was precious to my friend I had acted as his dresser before setting to work to remove my own make-up. There were two entrances to the establishment, by one of which Sherlock Holmes invariably entered and invariably went out, and from the other of which "Bill Jones" was sometimes seen to emerge, but never Sherlock Holmes. That my friend had made good his retirement I knew, but, nevertheless, if I had to open the door of the outer room it must be as "Jim."

Thinking it impolite not to do so, since the one who knocked might be aware that we had come in but not gone out again, I hastily readjusted that side of my moustache which I had begun to remove, replaced my cap and muffler, and carefully locking the door of the dressing-room, crossed the outer apartment and opened the door.

It was Holmes's custom never to enter or leave these rooms except under the mantle of friendly night, but at so early an hour I confess I had not expected a visitor. Wondering whom I should find there I opened the door.

Standing on the landing was a fellow-lodger who permanently occupied the two top rooms of the house. Sherlock Holmes had taken the trouble to investigate the man's past, for "Captain Dan," the name by which he was known in the saloons and worse resorts which he frequented, was palpably a broken-down gentleman; a piece of flotsam caught in the Oriental stream. Opium had been his downfall. How he lived I never knew, but Holmes believed he had some small but settled income, sufficient to enable him to kill himself in comfort with the black pills.

As he stood there before me in the early morning light, I was aware of some subtle change in his appearance. It was fully six months since I had seen him last, but in some vague way he looked younger. Haggard he was, with an ugly cut showing on his temple, but not so lined as I remembered him. Some former man seemed to be struggling through the opium-scarred surface. His eyes were brighter, and I noted with surprise that he wore decent clothes and was clean shaved.

"Good morning, Jim," he said; "you remember me, don't you?"

As he spoke I observed, too, that his manner had altered. He who had consorted with the sweepings af the doss-houses now addressed me as a courteous gentleman addresses an inferior — not haughtily or patronizingly, but with a note of conscious superiority and self-respect wholly unfamiliar. Almost it threw me off my guard, but remembering in the nick of time that I was still "Jim":

"Of course I remember you, Cap'n," I said. "Step inside."

"Thanks," he replied, and followed me into the little room.

I placed for him the armchair which our friend the fireman had so recently occupied, but:

"I won't sit down," he said.

And now I observed that he was evidently in a condition of repressed excitement. Perhaps he saw the curiosity in my glance, for he suddenly rested both his hands on my shoulders.

"Yes, I have given up the dope, Jim," he said — " done with it for ever. There's not a soul in this neighbourhood I can trust, yet if ever a man wanted a pal, I want one to-day. Now, you're square, my lad. I always knew that, in spite of the dope; and if I ask you to do a little thing that means a lot to me, I think you will do it. Am I right?"

"If it can be done, I'll do it," said I.

"Then, listen. I'm leaving England in the Patna for Singapore. She sails at noon to-morrow, and passengers go on board at ten o'clock. I've got my ticket, papers in order, but" — he paused impressively, grasping my shoulders hard — "I must get on board to-night."

I stared him in the face.

"Why?" I asked.

He returned my look with one searching and eager; then:

"If I show you the reason," said he, "and trust you with all my papers, will you go down to the dock — it's no great distance — and ask to see Marryat, the chief officer? Perhaps you've sailed with him?"

"No," I replied guardedly. "I was never in the Patna."

"Never mind. When you give him a letter which I shall write he will make the necessary arrangements for me to occupy my state-room to-night. I knew him well," he explained, "in — the old days. Will you do it, Jim?"

"I'll do it with pleasure," I answered.

"Shake!" said Captain Dan.

We shook hands heartily.

"Now I'll show you the reason," he added. "Come upstairs."

Turning, he led the way upstairs to his own room, and wondering greatly, I followed him in. Never having been in Captain Dan's apartments I cannot say whether they, like their occupant, had changed for the better. But I found myself in a room surprisingly clean and with a note of culture in its appointments which was even more surprising.

On a couch by the window, wrapped in a fur rug, lay the prettiest half-caste girl I had ever seen, East or West. Her skin was like cream rose petals and her abundant hair was of wonderful lustrous black. Perhaps it was her smooth warm colour which suggested the idea, but as her cheeks flushed at sight of Captain Dan and the long dark eyes lighted up in welcome, I thought of a delicate painting on ivory and I wondered more and more what it all could mean.

"I have brought Jim to see you," said Captain Dan. "No, don't trouble to move dear."

But even before he had spoken I had seen the girl wince with pain as she had endeavoured to sit up to greet us. She lay on her side in a rather constrained attitude, but although her sudden movement had brought tears to her eyes she smiled bravely and extended a tiny ivory hand to me.

"This is my wife, Jim!" said Captain Dan.

I could find no words at all, but merely stood there looking very awkward and feeling almost awed by the indescribable expression of trust in the eyes of the little Eurasian, as with her tiny fingers hidden in her husband's clasp she lay looking up at him.

"Now you know, Jim," said he, "why we must get aboard the Patna to-night. My wife is really too ill to travel; in fact, I shall have to carry her down to the cab, and such a proceeding in daylight would attract an enormous crowd in this neighbourhood!"

"Give me the letters and the papers," I answered. "I will start now."

His wife disengaged her hand and extended it to me.

"Thank you," she said, in a queer little silver-bell voice; "you are good. I shall always love you."

IV.

THE SECRET OF MA LORENZO

It must have been about eleven o'clock that night when Sherlock Holmes rang me up. Since we had parted in the early morning I had had no word from him, and I was all anxiety to tell him of the quaint little romance which unknown to us had had its setting in the room above.

In accordance with my promise I had seen the chief officer of the Patna; and from the start of surprise which he gave on opening "Captain Dan's" letter, I judged that Mr. Marryat and the man who for so long had sunk to the lowest rung of the ladder had been close friends in those "old days." At any rate, he had proceeded to make the necessary arrangements without a moment's delay, and the couple were to go on board the Patna at nine o'clock.

It was with a sense of having done at least one good deed that I finally quitted our Limehouse base and returned to my rooms. Now, at eleven o'clock at night:

"Can you come round to Baker Street at once?" said Holmes. "I want you to run down to Pennyfields with me."

"Some development in the Kwen Lung business?"

"Hardly a development, but I'm not satisfied, Watson. I hate to be beaten."

Twenty minutes later I was sitting in Holmes's study, watching him restlessly promenading up and down before the fire.

"The police searched Kwen Lung's place from foundation to tiles," he said. "I was there myself. Old Kwen Lung conveniently kept out of the way — still playing fan-tan, no doubt! But Ma Lorenzo was in evidence. She blandly declared that Kwen Lung never had a daughter! And in the absence of our friend the fireman, who sailed in the Seahawk, and whose evidence, by the way, is legally valueless — what could we do? They could find nobody in the neighbourhood prepared to state that Kwen Lung had a daughter or that Kwen Lung had no daughter. There are all sorts of fables about the old fox, but the facts about him are harder to get at."

"But," I explained, "the bloodstains on the Chinese idol!"

"Ma Lorenzo stumbled and fell there on the previous night, striking her skull against the foot of the figure."

"What nonsense!" I cried. "We should have seen the wound last night."

"We might have done," said Holmes musingly; "I don't know when she inflicted it on herself; but I did see it this morning."

"What!"

"Oh, the gash is there all right, partly covered by her hair."

He stood still, staring at me oddly.

"One meets with cases of singular devotion in unexpected quarters sometimes," he said.

"You mean that the woman inflicted the wound upon herself in order — "

"To save old Kwen Lung — exactly! It's marvellous."

"Good heavens!" I exclaimed. "And the window?"

"Oh! it was broken right enough — by two drunken sailormen fighting in the court outside! Sash and everything smashed to splinters."

He began irritably to pace the carpet again.

"It must have been a devil of a fight!" he added savagely.

"Meanwhile," said I, "where is old Kwen Lung hiding?"

"But more particularly," cried Holmes, "where has he hidden the poor victim? Come along, Watson! I'm going down there for a final look round."

"Of course the premises are being watched?"

"Of course — and also, of course, I shall be the laughing stock of Scotland Yard if nothing results."

It was close on midnight when once more I found myself in Pennyfields. Carried away by Holmes's irritable excitement, I had quite forgotten the romance of Captain Dan; and when, having exchanged greetings with the detective on duty hard by the house of Kwen Lung, we presently found ourselves in the presence of Ma Lorenzo, I scarcely knew for a moment if I were "Jim" or my proper self.

"Is Kwen Lung in?" asked Holmes sternly.

The woman shook her head.

"No," she replied; "he sometimes stop away a whole week."

"Does he?" jerked Holmes. "Come in, Watson; we'll take another look round."

A moment later I found myself again in the room of the golden Chinese idol. The red curtain had been removed from before the shattered window, but otherwise the place looked exactly as it had looked before. The atmosphere was much less stale, however, but there was something repellent about the great gilded idol smiling eternally from his pedestal beside the door.

I stared into the leering face, and it was the face of one who knew and who might have said: "Yes! this and other things equally strange have I beheld in many lands as well as England. Much I could tell. Many things grim and terrible, and some few joyous; for behold! I smile but am silent."

For a while Holmes stared abstractedly at the bloodstains on the pedestal of the Chinese idol and upon the floor beneath from which the matting had been pulled back. Suddenly he turned to Ma Lorenzo:

"Where have you hidden the body?" he demanded.

Watching her, I thought I saw the woman flinch, but there was enough of the Oriental in her composition to save her from self-betrayal. She shook her head slowly, watching Holmes through half-closed eyes.

"Nobody hab," she replied.

And I thought for once that her lapse into pidgin had been deliberate and not accidental.

When finally we quitted the house of the missing Kwen Lung, and when, Holmes having curtly acknowledged "good night" from the detective on duty, we came out into Limehouse Causeway.

"You have not overlooked the possibility, Holmes," I said, "that this woman's explanation may be true, and that the fireman of the Seahawk may have been entertaining us with an account of a weird dream?"

"No!" snapped Holmes — "neither will Scotland Yard overlook it."

He was in a particularly impossible mood, for he so rarely made mistakes that to be detected in one invariably brought out those petulant traits of character which may have been due in some measure to long residence in the East. Recognizing that he would rather be alone I parted from him at the corner of Baker Street and returned to my own chambers. Furthermore, I was very tired, for it was close upon two o'clock, and on turning in I very promptly went to sleep, nor did I awaken until late in the morning.

For some odd reason, but possibly because the fact had occurred to me just as I was retiring, I remembered at the moment of waking that I had not told Holmes about the romantic wedding of Captain Dan. As I had left my friend in very ill humour I thought that this would be a good excuse for an early call, and just before eleven o'clock I walked into his office. Innes, his invaluable secretary, showed me into the study at the back.

"Hallo, Watson," said Holmes, looking up from a little silver Buddha which he was examining, "have you come to ask for news of the Kwen Lung case?"

"No," I replied. "Is there any?"

Holmes shook his head.

"It seems like fate," he declared, "that this thing should have been sent to me this morning." He indicated the silver Buddha. "A present from a friend who knows my weakness for Chinese ornaments," he explained grimly. "It reminds me of that damned Chinese idol of Kwen Lung's!"

I took up the little image and examined it with interest. It was most beautifully fashioned in the patient Oriental way, and there was a little hinged door in the back which fitted so perfectly that when closed it was quite impossible to detect its presence. I glanced at Holmes.

"I suppose you didn't find a jewel inside?" I said lightly.

"No," he replied; "there was nothing inside."

But even as he uttered the words his whole expression changed, and so suddenly as to startle me. He sprang up from the table.

"Have you an hour to spare, Watson?" he cried excitedly.

"I can spare an hour, but what for?"

"For Kwen Lung!"

Four minutes later we were speeding in the direction of Limehouse, and not a word of explanation to account for this sudden journey could I extract from my friend. Therefore I beguiled the time by telling him of my adventure with Captain Dan.

Holmes listened to the story in unbroken silence, but at its termination he brought his hand down sharply on my knee.

"I have been almost perfectly blind, Watson," he said; "but not quite so perfectly blind as you!"

I stared at him in amazement, but he merely laughed and offered no explanation of his words.

Presently, then, I found myself yet again in the familiar room of the golden Chinese idol. Ma Lorenzo, in whom some hidden anxiety seemed to have increased since I had last seen her, stood at the top of the stairs watching us. Upon what idea my friend was operating and what he intended to do I could not imagine; but without a word to the woman he crossed the room and grasping the great golden idol with both arms he dragged it forward across the floor!

As he did so there was a stifled shriek, and Ma Lorenzo, stumbling down the steps, threw herself on her knees before Holmes! Raising imploring hands:

"No, no!" she moaned. "Not until I tell you — I tell you everything first!"

"To begin with, tell me how to open this thing," he said sternly.

Momentarily she hesitated, and did not rise from her knees, but:

"Do you hear me?" he cried.

The woman rose unsteadily and walking slowly round the Chinese idol manipulated some hidden fastening, whereupon the entire back of the thing opened like a door! From what was within she shudderingly averted her face, but Holmes, stepping back against the wall, stopped and peered into the cavity.

"Good God!" he muttered. "Come and look, Watson."

Prepared by his manner for some gruesome spectacle, I obeyed — and from that which I saw I recoiled in horror.

"Holmes," I whispered, "Holmes! who is it?"

The spectacle had truly sickened me. Crouched within the narrow space enclosed by the figure of the idol was the body of an old and wrinkled Chinaman! His knees were drawn up to his chin, and his head so compressed upon them that little of his features could be seen.

"It is Kwen Lung!" murmured Ma Lorenzo, standing with clasped hands and wild eyes over by the window. "Kwen Lung — and I am glad he is dead!"

Such a note of hatred came into her voice as I had never heard in the voice of any woman.

"He is vile, a demon, a mocking cruel demon! Long, long years ago I would have killed him, but always I was afraid. I tell you everything, everything. This is how he comes to be dead. The little one" — again her voice changed and a note of almost grotesque tenderness came into it — "the lotus-flower, that is his own daughter's child, flesh of his flesh, he keeps a prisoner as the women of China are kept, up there" — she raised one fat finger aloft — "up above. He does not know that someone comes to see her — someone who used to come to smoke but who gave it up because he had looked into the dear one's eye. He does not know that she goes with me to see her man. Ah! we think he does not know! I — I arrange it all. A week ago they were married. Tuesday night, when Kwen Lung die, I plan for her to steal away for ever, for ever."

Tears now were running down the woman's fat cheeks, and her voice quivered emotionally.

"For me it is the end, but for her it is the beginning of life. All right! I don't matter a damn! She is young and beautiful. Ah, God! so beautiful! A drunken pig comes here and finds his way in, so I give him the smoke and presently he sleeps, but it makes delay, and I don't know how soon Kwen Lung, that Oriental demon, will wake. For he is like the bats who sleep all day and wake at night.

"At last the sailor pig sleeps and I call softly to my dear little one that the time has come. I have gone out into the street, locking the door behind me, to see if her man is waiting, and I hear her shrieks — her shrieks! I hurry back. My hands tremble so much that I can scarcely unlock the door. At last I enter, and I see and I know — that Oriental devil has learned all and has been playing with us like cat and mouse! He is lashing her, with a great whip! Lashing her — that tiny, sweet flower. Ah!"

She choked in her utterance, and turning to the gilded Chinese idol which contained the dead Chinaman she shook her clenched hands at it, and the expression on her face I can never forget. Then:

"As I shriek curses at him, crash goes the window — and I see her husband spring into the room! The tender one had fallen, there at the foot of the Chinese idol, and Kwen Lung, his teeth gleaming — like a rat — like a devil — turns to meet him. So he is when her man strike him, once. Just once, here." She rested her hand upon her heart. "And he falls — and he coughs. He lie still. For him it is finished. That devil heart has ceased to beat. Ah!"

She threw up her hands.

"That is all. I tell you no more."

"One thing more," said Holmes sternly; "the name of the man who killed Kwen Lung?"

At that Ma Lorenzo slowly raised her head and folded her arms across her bosom. There was something one could never forget in the expression of her fat face.

"Not if you burn me alive!" she answered in a low voice. "No one ever knows that — from me."

She sank on to the divan and buried her face in her hands. Her fat shoulders shook grotesquely; and Holmes stood perfectly still staring across at her for fully a minute. I could hear voices in the street outside and the hum of traffic in Limehouse Causeway.

Then my friend did a singular thing. Walking over to the gilded Chinese idol he reclosed the opening and not without a great effort pushed the great idol back against the wall.

"There are times, Watson," he said, staring at me oddly, "when I'm glad that I am not an official agent of the law."

While I watched him dumfounded he walked across to the woman and touched her on the shoulder. She raised her tear-stained face.

"All right," she whispered. "I am ready."

"Get ready as soon as you like," said he tersely.

"I'll have the man removed who is watching the house, and you can reckon on forty-eight hours to make yourself scarce."

With never another word he seized me by the arm and hurried me out of the place! Ten paces along the street a shabby-looking fellow was standing, leaning against a pillar. Holmes stopped.

"Even the greatest men make mistakes sometimes, Hewitt," he remarked. "I'm throwing up the case; probably Inspector Wessex will do the same. Good morning."

On towards the Causeway he led me — for not a word was I capable of uttering; and just before we reached that artery of Chinatown, from down-river came the deep, sustained note of a steamer's siren, the warning of some big liner leaving dock.

"That will be the Patna," said Holmes. "She sails at twelve o'clock, I think you said?"

THE END

EDITOR'S NOTES

In the late 1800s and early 1900s, at the peak of Sherlock Holmes' popularity, a number of writers wrote their own mystery stories that were in many ways similar to Holmes. Many of Sax Rohmer's little-known stories read, but for the names and places, almost exactly like Arthur Conan Doyle's original Sherlock Holmes stories — in fact, much of the language is more like the original Holmes canon than most stories written by modern authors. Rohmer was also a much better writer than many of the other "Rivals of Sherlock Holmes" authors.

The editor of this volume has carefully edited some of Rohmer's best Chinatown tales into Sherlock Holmes pastiches. The stories are set during the time and after Holmes's retirement to keep bees on the Susex Downs.

Many modern authors have attempted to recapture the nostalgic mood of gaslit London and the mystique of Conan Doyle's adventures of Sherlock Holmes by writing "new" Holmes stories; yet these attempts frequently fail to capture the original flavor of the Conan Doyle tales because modern writers simply don't think or speak like Victorians.

In the late 1800s and early 1900s, at the peak of Sherlock Holmes' popularity, a number of mystery writers wrote stories of their own which were in many ways similar to Sherlock Holmes. Conan Doyle's contemporaries wrote characters of their own invention; nevertheless they sound more like Conan Doyle than do any writers today.

Many of Sax Rohmer's little-known stories read, but for the names and places, almost exactly like Arthur Conan Doyle's

Sherlock Holmes tales — in fact, much of the language is more like the original Holmes canon than stories written by any other author.

Unlike Sir Arthur's modern imitators, Sax Rohmer wrote stories at the time Conan Doyle was at the peak of his popularity; and there is a ring of authenticity in Rohmer's narratives that modern imitators are lacking. Sax Rohmer was also a much better writer than many of the other contemporary "Rivals of Sherlock Holmes" authors.

The editor of this volume has carefully revised some of Rohmer's best Chinatown tales into Sherlock Holmes pastiches. These stories are set after Holmes' return from his retirement to assist the British Government in the WWI era.

— Alan Lance Andersen

Pastiches

After the invention of the detective mystery format in 1841 by Edgar Allan Poe, there were a large number of Victorian and Edwardian writers in both England and America who began writing detective mystery stories — for this was the era when Arthur Conan Doyle was creating Sherlock Holmes tales on a regular basis in *Strand* Magazine. And detective stories were very profitable financially. Many of the "period" writers intentionally imitated Conan Doyle's characters and story formula.

Modern authors from John Dickson Carr to Nicholas Meyer and Steven Philip Jones have attempted to recapture the mood of gaslit London and the mystique of Conan Doyle's adventures of Sherlock Holmes by writing "new" Holmes novels and short stories; yet these attempts frequently fail to capture the original flavor of the Conan Doyle tales, because modern writers simply don't think or speak like Victorians.

On the other hand, Conan Doyle's contemporaries — such mystery authors as Robert Eustace, L.T. Meade, Clifford Halifax, Sax Rohmer, and Richard Harding Davis — were writing about characters of their own invention; nevertheless they sound more like Conan Doyle than do any of his deliberate modern imitators. One of the more successful of these "period" writers was Sax Rohmer, whose stories were as familiar to readers of *Colliers* Magazine as the Sherlock Holmes was to *Strand*.

Unlike Sir Arthur's modern imitators, Sax Rohmer wrote his stories at the time Conan Doyle was at the peak of his popularity; and there is a ring of authenticity in Rohmer's narratives that modern imitatorsare lacking. Originally, Rohmer's stories used different character names — due to Conan Doyle's copyright protection. But now in 2016, both Sax Rohmer's stories and the Sherlock Holmes canon are all in the public domain. Thus it is now possible to present ... Sax Rohmer's version of Sherlock Holmes. The editor of this volume has carefully edited some of Rohmer's best mystery tales into Sherlock Holmes pastiches.

Literary historian John Kennedy Melling, author of *Murder Done to Death: A Survey of Parody and Pastiche in Crime Fiction,* says of *The Affairs of Sherlock Holmes*:

"Writing pastiches successfully involves loving your subject and his life and knowing every detail of his world. The editor of this book has experience in radio, conjuring, and interactive theatre — which ensures that these stories will intrigue new readers without upsetting original Sherlock Holmes aficionados. In THE AFFAIRS OF SHERLOCK HOLMES, the adaptation of Sax Rohmer's larger-than-life characters and distinctive style to the Sherlock Holmes purview triumphantly fills the pages of this intriguing book."

— Alan Lance Andersen

SAX ROHMER

(Born: February 15, 1883 – Died: June 1, 1959).

Sax Rohmer was the pen name of Arthur Henry Sarsfield Ward He worked as a poet, songwriter, and comedy sketch writer in Music Halls before creating the Sax Rohmer persona and pursuing a career writing weird fiction.

In 1911, Rohmer's first "Fu Manchu" novel, *The Mystery of Dr. Fu-Manchu*, was published, along with magazine serialization from October 1912 to June 1913. It was an immediate success, with its fast-paced story of Denis Nayland Smith and Dr. Petrie facing the worldwide conspiracy of the 'Yellow Peril.'

The Fu Manchu stories — together with his more conventional detective series characters: Paul Harley, Gaston Max, Red Kerry, The Crime Magnet, and Morris Klaw (an occult detective) — made Rohmer one of the most successful and well-paid authors of the 1920s and 1930s.

Rohmer was friends with Harry Houdini and based his crime-solving magician Bazarada on the great escape artist. Rohmer included a fictionalized version of the infamous Aleister Crowley as the arch-villain in one Bazarada story.

Rohmer's meeting and romantic love affair with long-suffering Rose Elizabeth Knox, who became his wife after a year-long star-crossed love misadventure, would make a marvelous subject for motion pictures or novel.

Also from MX Publishing

MX Publishing is the world's largest specialist Sherlock Holmes publisher, with over two hundred titles and one hundred authors creating the latest in Sherlock Holmes fiction and non-fiction.

From traditional short stories and novels to travel guides and quiz books, MX Publishing cater for all Holmes fans.

The collection includes leading titles such as *Benedict Cumberbatch In Transition* and *The Norwood Author* which won the 2011 Howlett Award (Sherlock Holmes Book of the Year).

MX Publishing also has one of the largest communities of Holmes fans on Facebook with regular contributions from dozens of authors.

www.mxpublishing.com

Also from MX Publishing

The Missing Authors Series

 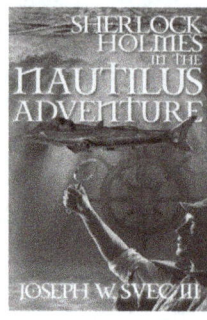 

Sherlock Holmes and The Adventure of The Grinning Cat
Sherlock Holmes and The Nautilus Adventure
Sherlock Holmes and The Round Table Adventure

"Joseph Svec, III is brilliant in entwining two endearing and enduring classics of literature, blending the factual with the fantastical; the playful with the pensive; and the mischievous with the mysterious. We shall, all of us young and old, benefit with a cup of tea, a tranquil afternoon, and a copy of Sherlock Holmes, The Adventure of the Grinning Cat."
Amador County Holmes Hounds Sherlockian Society

www.mxpublishing.com

Also from MX Publishing

The Detective and The Woman Series

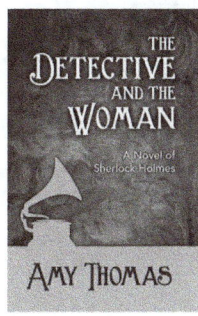  

The Detective and The Woman
The Detective, The Woman and The Winking Tree
The Detective, The Woman and The Silent Hive

"The book is entertaining, puzzling and a lot of fun. I believe the author has hit on the only type of long-term relationship possible for Sherlock Holmes and Irene Adler. The details of the narrative only add force to the romantic defects we expect in both of them and their growth and development are truly marvelous to watch. This is not a love story. Instead, it is a coming-of-age tale starring two of our favorite characters."
Philip K Jones

www.mxpublishing.com